Frank waves a finger at the Pryce pictures she's propped against an empty flower vase.

"You were holding out on me," she tells the children. "You knew that all along. Naughty kids. How am I supposed to find the bad guy if you won't work with me?"

Frank has taken to animated conversations with the mute, smiling faces. In a more talkative person the habit might be amusing. Contrasted against Frank's natural reticence, the trait is ominous. Heedless of the portent, she circles the dining room tables, damaging as much of a fifth as she can before going to Gail's.

She's come to dread the hours of her leaving. Gail has become an image on the periphery of Frank's vision, an annoying shadow that will neither go away nor come into focus. Gail deserves more than her slightly besotted and grudging tolerance, but that's the best Frank can muster these days. She tells herself her apathy will pass, that someday she'll be able to see Gail clearly again and will remember why she fell in love with the doc. But for the moment, memory eludes her.

Visit

Bella Books

at

BellaBooks.com

or call our toll-free number

1-800-729-4992

LAST CALL

Baxter CLARE

Bella
BOOKS

2004

Bella Books, Inc.
P.O. Box 10543
Tallahassee, FL 32302

Printed in the United States of America on acid-free paper
First Edition

Editor: Christi Cassidy
Cover designer: Sandy Knowles

ISBN 1-931513-70-8

For Lance and Lovey
and every joyful hour

ABOUT THE AUTHOR

Baxter Clare lives in Central California with her spouse, artist Anno O'Connor. In additon to writing novels, she holds a Master's Degree in Biology and works as a wildlife biologist. She is the author of a non-fiction work, *Spirit of the Valley* (written as Baxter Trautman), and three previous L.A. Franco mysteries. She is at work on her fifth novel.

Chapter 1

Lieutenant L.A. Franco's message is short: "Noah, you lazy bastard, where are you? Give me a call."

She hangs up on Noah Jantzen's voice mail, wondering why her cop has missed the Monday morning six AM briefing. That's not like him. He's usually early, not late. She wonders if one of the kids is sick. By eight o'clock Frank is worried enough to call his wife. The receptionist transfers the call to Tracey Jantzen's ward. A man named Eric answers.

"Eric, could I speak to Tracey Jantzen, please."

"Uh, she's not here."

"Will she be in later?"

"Uh, no. She came in but she had to leave."

Frank stops filling out a requisition form. She's spent a career listening to bullshit and she's hearing it now. She puts down her pen and says, "Eric. My name's Lieutenant Franco. Tracey's husband

1

works for me. I'm trying to locate either him or Tracey. Do you know where I can get in touch with her?"

"Um, I think her husband was in some kind of accident. She went flying out of here. She didn't say where she was going but I guess she's with him."

"All right," Frank says. Ice water replaces blood in her veins. She speaks with extreme deliberation, as if the man on the phone was a five-year-old. "Eric, it's critical I find her. She has a cell phone. I need you, or your supervisor, to find that number for me. Do you understand?"

"Yeah, sure. Hang on a sec."

The phone gets quiet in her ear and Frank yells, "Lewis!"

A large, ebony woman appears in Frank's office.

"Go through Noah's desk and find Tracey Jantzen's cell phone number."

Frank is sure Noah knew his wife's number by heart but hopes he's got it written down somewhere.

A woman says into Frank's ear, "This is Amanda Koening. How can I help you?"

Frank prays for Amanda Koening's sake that she doesn't want to play hardball.

"Ms. Koening," Frank starts.

Lewis comes in and hands Frank a scrap of paper. Frank hangs up. She dials the number Lewis gave her. It rings once, twice, three times. Four times. Five. Tracey answers on the sixth ring. Her voice is thin and Frank's guts get loose.

"Trace. It's Frank. Where are you?"

Frank is moving even as Tracey sobs. "Oh, Frank, I'm at L.A. County. Come quick. It's bad."

Chapter 2

Waiting for the doctor, Frank wonders, if karma is true, what the hell has she done in past lives that she has to watch so many people die in this one? Who was she? Hitler? Pol Pot?

She and Tracey try to reassure each other with valiant bravado. When the doctor comes out they stop pretending. The doctor is a woman, and maybe because of that she spares them a lot of the details, stating simply that when Noah was crushed against the steering column he suffered massive pulmonary trauma and they just couldn't stop the bleeding. His heart stopped and they couldn't get it going again. Of course she was very sorry.

As Tracey starts screaming Frank reaches for her, saying singsong in her head, *All the king's horses, and all the king's men, couldn't put Noah together again.*

She accompanies Tracey to the operating room, stopping at the door. Frank's played this scene before. Her mind and feet won't move her closer to the metal altar where her best friend lies broken under an obscenely white sheet. Frank stares at the litter of useless offerings—plastic tubing and torn wrappers, discarded gloves, footprints smeared in Noah's blood. She listens to Tracey's simultaneous vilifying and deifying, her outrage against this final and most unjust of decisions. Frank absorbs every detail, feeling herself detach from the trauma like a balloon cut from its tether.

When Tracey returns to Frank's arms she moans about how to tell the kids. Frank guides her from the building, letting Tracey cry and stumble against her. It takes them a while to find the car, then Frank drives Tracey home. When Tracey is calmed enough, Frank has her call her sister. Frank will stay with Tracey until the sister comes. She offers to pick the kids up but suggests Tracey let them finish their day in school. Their world will crumble soon enough. Let them have a few more hours of ignorant bliss. Tracey agrees and when the sister comes, Frank calls a cab.

In the taxi, she calls the station and talks to Diego. She tells him to bring in whoever's not in the squad room and to stay until she gets there. She hangs up and closes her eyes.

Maybe she's just having a really fucked-up dream.

Frank probes the edges of reality. Traffic sounds through the window and the taxi jolts to a stop. The driver has the AC on too high and the cab is sour from the sweat of thousands of bodies. When Frank opens her eyes, she is disappointed, but not surprised, to see that nothing has changed. She rolls the window down, preferring the hot sting of tar and diesel to the cab's fetid cold air.

The driver drops her off at the hospital and she sits in her car, buying time. When she finally starts the engine, she drives slowly to the Figueroa Station. Her station. Noah's station. The only division either of them has ever worked. They partnered on the street and later again in homicide. They never got arbitrarily transferred and never put in for a move. Newton, Figueroa, Rampart—those are the stations that rookies without connections get assigned to and bad cops get demoted to. Frank had been put there straight out of the academy and Noah had transferred in from Pacific when he got off probation. He complained about his choice from then on but never did anything to change it. Noah was a whiner. He didn't mean most of what he said, but it was how he dealt with life. Frank had learned to ignore him or tease him. Usually the latter. Humor was Noah's other coping tool, and he made Frank laugh, too.

Climbing the stairs to the homicide room, she wonders who'll make her laugh now.

Faces question her when she walks into the room. Bobby, Jill, Lewis, Diego, Johnnie, Darcy—their presence makes Noah's absence grossly conspicuous. For a horrifying instant Frank feels her heart ripping open. She stares at the floor, willing herself to do what she must. A tsunami of grief breaks over her, then washes back to the far horizon from which it came. Frank lifts her head.

"Noah was in an accident on the way to work. Three-car pileup. He suffered major internal damage. They couldn't stop the bleeding."

The phone rings. No one moves to pick it up. Jill finally has the courage to ask, "He's dead?"

"Yeah."

Then they break. Jill cries. Bobby and Diego turn to their desks. Johnnie swears and fires questions at Frank. She doesn't know the answer to one, doesn't see the relevance of the other, but answers anyway. Lewis stares at her big hands and Darcy fidgets with a Pepsi can.

Frank addresses them. "You can take the rest of the day off if you want. It's up to you. I'll cover."

It's Bobby who follows her into her office, his dark face lit with concern. "What about Tracey?"

Frank explains.

"What about the funeral? Is there a date?"

A strange impulse to anger rises in Frank. Instead of yelling, "Jesus Christ! The bastard's barely four hours cold," she answers, "I'll let you know as soon as I find out."

When Bobby leaves, she does a rare thing and tells him to close the door. She has more calls to make.

The hardest is her old lieutenant. Noah's old lieutenant. There's never a good time to call Joe Girardi. The time zone puts them two hours apart and usually when Frank thinks to call him it's in the middle of his dinner or after he's in bed. In the morning he's out on the lake. In the afternoon he takes a nap. Evenings he's at one of his damn AA meetings. There will never be a good time for this call, but she can't put it off.

Ruth, Joe's third wife, answers. She sounds pleased to hear from Frank, a change that occurred only after her husband retired. She tells Frank to wait, Joe's outside. Frank blows loudly into the telephone, massaging the back of her neck. Joe comes on, chirping, "Hey, hey, girlie-girl. Give us the report from the trenches."

Frank gives it to him straight up. She hears sorrow in his response, acknowledges it without reciprocating. Spending his days fishing on Lake Superior, Joe can afford this luxurious dip into emotion. He is well removed from its constant ravages. Frank is not. She is deep in the thick of it. One misstep and she'll drown in it like a common civilian. Not an option.

Frank kneads the knots below her skull while Joe asks how Tracey and the kids are holding up.

"As well as can be expected," she answers.

"How about you? How you doing?"

She says, "Fine," too quickly.

Joe waits for more. When there isn't any, his response is as measured as the footsteps of a man in a minefield. "Are you still seeing that shrink over at the BSU?"

"No. He retired. I'm all right. Really."

"Okay," Joe says, sounding unconvinced. "When's the funeral?"

"I'm not sure yet. I'll let you know. Think you can make it?"

"Oh, I'll make it."

"Good. Listen I just wanted to let you know. Wanted you to hear it from me. I'll call you as soon as Tracey sets a date."

"Sure, sure. I appreciate the call, Frank. I know it was a hard one to make."

"Yeah. Get back to those fish."

Frank gently replaces the receiver. Then she hurls the phone across the room. It breaks into dozens of pieces. Frank wants to throw more.

Chapter 3

Everyone is out of the office by two, including Frank. She cannot wait to leave today. Usually the office is her sanctuary, her refuge from the world, but today it mocks her. Everything in it reminds her of Noah.

She grabs a six-pack at Cat's Liquors. Two bottles are gone before she reaches the Alibi. She is sure Johnnie will be at the bar and doesn't know if she can face his pain. He partnered with Noah for a long time after Frank became lieutenant. He and Noah fought like they were married, but they covered for each other too. Johnnie hated it when Frank paired Noah with Lewis, but Noah'd been ready for the change and eager to coach the prickly detective trainee.

Frank parks outside the Alibi but doesn't shut the car off. There will be other cops in there. As the afternoon changes to evening, people from Parker Center and the district attorney's office will trickle in. Frank doesn't want to deal with their sad faces and so sorry's. She keeps driving. She gets onto the freeway and heads north. She catches the 210 to Lincoln Avenue. Traffic is light and soon she's climbing into the San Gabriel Mountains.

She remembers an overlook that looks down on Pasadena. She finds it vacant and pulls in. Taking her fourth beer, she sits on the hood. The engine ticks beneath her. A warm breeze lifts her hair. She looks down at the city while the sun kisses her arms. For a moment she is almost peaceful, but the day returns and being up here is no good either. She wants to run. To get in the car and keep driving, but where to? There's nowhere to go. Frank doesn't know what to do with pain like this, except drown it. Drown it even as she denies its existence.

She guzzles the beer and waits for the click. The click that Brick explains in *Cat on a Hot Tin Roof*. The click in his head that switches the hot light off and the cool one on. The click that makes him feel peaceful.

But the click doesn't happen. It's too soon and she knows it. Before she reaches for the fifth beer, she hurls her empty into the brush. She chases it with a wild, gargled yell, slamming both fists against the hood, but her pain remains unfazed.

When the six-pack is gone she goes home, stopping on the way for a bottle of Scotch. She's supposed to be at her lover's tonight. It's the regular routine—a couple weeknights, and weekends, spent at Gail Lawless's apartment—but when the doc calls, she lets her talk to the answering machine. Frank digs deep for the strength to tell Gail what's happened. Clinging to her glass of Black Label, her shovel, she returns the call.

"Hi."

"Hi yourself. Where are you?"

"Home."

"Are you on your way over?"

"Nope."

"How come?" The pause is long enough that Gail asks, "What's wrong?"

Gail waits until Frank can say, "Noah's dead. Car wreck on his way in this morning."

Frank hears the sharp intake of breath. She dreads what's coming next but bears the standard response stoically. Nor does she protest when Gail says, "I'm coming over."

Gail lets herself in and crosses the room to where Frank is leaning against the patio door. She enfolds Frank and Frank dutifully accepts the embrace. Gail's smell is sweet and familiar, as wonderful as a child's must be to its mother. Frank has loved the scent of this woman, the feel of her flesh against hers, but for all the comfort it brings tonight, she may as well be hugging marble. She feels nothing and that's all right. The click is kicking in. While she wouldn't exactly say it was peaceful, at least it isn't painful. And that is worth a lot. Yes, indeed, that is plenty good right now and she won't risk losing that precious cessation of feeling.

The doc asks, "How'd you find out?"

"When he hadn't called in by eight I tracked Tracey down at County General."

"What happened to him?"

"I told you. He was in a car accident."

"No, I mean, was it his head, internal trauma?"

Irritation bleeds into Frank's drunken equanimity but she decides the question is only natural coming from the county coroner. "He bled out. The doctor working on him said he'd sustained a lot of trauma and that they couldn't stop the bleeding. His heart quit."

Frank's almost stops as she says that. *Noah's heart quit.* She can't believe that big, stupid, goofy heart could be stilled. How could an organ with so much life in it just quit? Her heart, sure. It was a rock. People like her died every day. That was to be expected. But Noah was *good*. He was a good dad, a good husband, a good cop. A good friend.

"Did you get to see him? Or talk to him?"

10

"No. He was in surgery when I got there. He never came out of it. Tracey didn't get to see him either. Not until it was over."

They have broken apart a little and Gail nods at the glass affixed to Frank's hand. "I assume you're getting drunk."

"Not as drunk as I'd like to. Fubar's on call, Darcy and Bobby volunteered to catch tonight, but I want to see Tracey first thing in the morning. I won't be any good to her hungover."

"How is she?"

"Pretty fucked up. Her sister's with her."

"Is there anything I can do?"

Frank shakes her head. "Nothing anybody can do."

"Have you eaten at all?"

"No."

"How about some soup?" Gail asks, moving toward the kitchen. Frank doesn't stop her.

"How'd everybody at work take it?"

Again Frank is irritated. It's taken her hours to dim the day's hot lights and Gail's flipping them back on.

"Like you'd expect. I gave 'em the choice to go home if they wanted. Johnnie and Jill left."

"What about Lewis?"

"She seemed kind of at odds." Then more to herself, Frank says, "I don't know what I'll do with her."

Cheryl Lewis had come into the 93rd Squad barely a year ago. Frank had watched her advance from boot to sergeant and when Frank needed replacements for her depleted squad, she'd requested Lewis. She'd partnered her with Noah. Lewis was big, black and temperamental. Noah was an impish, skinny, white boy whom Lewis insisted on calling O'Malley even though he always countered he was Jewish. Noah would take his partner to the edge of her temper and back away, gradually building elasticity into it. Lewis learned quickly and Noah blossomed as a mentor. He was a helluva good cop. Frank had always thought if the day came when she was ready to leave the nine-three that she'd like to leave Noah holding the reins.

Now that won't happen.

Gail puts a bowl of tomato soup on the table and Frank sits in front of it. She tastes a few spoonfuls, then lets the soup cool and drinks her Scotch. Gail gazes at her over the slab of glass tabletop.

"How are you?" she asks, chin in hand.

Frank pushes the bowl aside and adopts the same pose. Gail is lovely. Green eyes, crow's feet, the silky, dark-chocolate pageboy that Frank only recently found out is dyed. All lovely. Frank would testify to it in a court of law, but Gail's beauty can't move her. She sees Gail from a great remove, like a master's painting in a book of great art.

"How am I?" Frank repeats, having no idea how to answer the question. "I guess I'm all right."

"How do you feel?"

Referring to the BSU shrink she used to see, Frank counters, "You sound like Clay."

"You liked Clay."

"Not in my living room."

A slight curve lifts Gail's lips. Frank realizes they didn't kiss hello. She wonders if it's too late. She could lean over and kiss the soft folds right now. She knows what they will feel like. Firm and giving at the same time. Frank considers this but doesn't have the inclination to act on it.

"How much of that have you had?" Gail asks, indicating the glass at Frank's elbow.

"I'm not counting."

Frank's "lapses into inebriation," as Gail calls them, are an issue around which they have created a wary détente. Gail's dad was a destructive drunk, always promising to go on the wagon and stay there, and always falling off. Frank doesn't get drunk in front of Gail and Gail doesn't bring it up. Today Frank has broken the rules and couldn't care less. Her best friend's dead and she's entitled. She lets the chips of their delicate truce fall where they may.

"Would you like me to stay?" Gail surprises Frank by adding, "I promise I won't nag."

Frank reaches across the table for her hand. "Yes."

She says this because she thinks it will please Gail to feel needed. Also because it's the right thing to say. One shouldn't be alone at times like this and all that jazz. What she won't admit is that, lying restlessly under fathoms of alcohol is the frail hope that Gail can touch her, that the doc can offer some small measure of comfort. That maybe, just maybe, Gail can become part of the click.

Chapter 4

The next morning, Frank is comforted by the distraction of a mild hangover. She stays at Tracey's long enough for a cup of coffee. Amid tears and dark laughter, Tracey, her sister and one of Noah's sisters are managing the funeral arrangements. Tracey's mom and dad are flying in this afternoon and Noah's folks will drive up tomorrow from San Diego. Tracey and the kids will be surrounded by people who love them, and Frank will stay out of the way.

Before leaving, Frank hugs Noah's kids. Leslie is just hitting puberty. She is silent and withdrawn. At ten, Jamie is wide-eyed and brave, vainly trying to comfort her baby brother. Markie is old enough to understand his father is dead, but young enough to burst into tears for him. She returns them to the diversion of aunts and cousins, making Tracey promise to call her if there is anything at all she needs.

The rest of Frank's morning is spent repeating the phone calls she made yesterday. Without emotion, she relays the details of Saturday's funeral and memorial. The squad drifts in and out, until they have all gone home, but Frank remains, burying herself in the minutiae of administration.

Now it is a few ticks shy of midnight. Frank paces the squad room. Her cadre of ghosts follows in close formation. Light filters in from her office and the hall. The squad room dozes, undisturbed by the station sounds drifting up the stairs.

Smoking is not permitted in the building yet a blue haze nuzzles the ceiling. Frank stops long enough to light a new cigarette off her old one. She drops the stub into the Pepsi can Darcy uses to spit his chew, the sizzling extinction pleasing her. From the boom box in her office, Sinatra spills his guts. The CD player was a birthday gift from the squad. She'd been touched, sure it had been Noah's idea to replace her ancient cassette player.

Frank keeps stopping at his desk. Like a kitchen is always the gathering place in a house, Noah's desk has always been the focal point of the office. The metal sides are upholstered with his kids' artwork held in place by a variety of magnets. Colorful paintings and poems paper the wall behind the desk. Noah updated the school photographs each year but never changed the picture of Tracey he put on his desk his first day in homicide. She picks up Tracey's smiling face. Frank used to joke that he wanted a younger wife, but Noah always maintained the picture was good luck.

"Not good enough," she tells the picture. She puts it down, continuing past the silent hulk. After a few more tours around the cramped office, Frank is inevitably drawn back to the desk. She stares at the cluttered top, then pulls Noah's chair out. She sits in it, pushing and prodding at papers. She will have to divvy his cases among the squad. Prominent on the desk is the murder book for a stabbing he caught two days ago. Lewis can have that. Noah is—*uh-uh*, Frank corrects herself. *Was*. Noah *was* the primary on it, and as his partner, Lewis has already helped him work it. Besides, Frank's sure that sooner or later someone will drop a dime on their perp.

Frank lifts the cover on another binder. The dead crack baby. Lewis can handle this one, too. There's a rock hound out there that carried for nine months and is suddenly childless. Lewis'll either find the woman who suffocated her infant or she'll get someone to talk. Life's cheap in South Central, but smothering a baby and burying it under a pile of garbage is scandalous even by 'hood standards.

Mentally parceling out Noah's cases, she leaves the murder books where they are. The mess on his desk is comforting. It lets her believe Noah's coming back, that he's just at home, on vacation, taking sick time. He'll be back. The work waiting for him tells her so.

Like faithful hounds by their master's chair, two cardboard file boxes press against the desk. A pile of obsolete memos and crinkled forms sit on top of them. And a shoebox.

"Oh, yeah," she mutters. The Pryce case. Was he working on it? Not likely, considering the boxes are covered with papers. Still, Frank checks a couple of the old memos. Their dates suggest the boxes haven't been touched in at least six weeks. She thinks back. It could have been slow enough then that he'd gone through the case one more time.

Almost seven years old, Pryce is still unsolved. Noah'd caught the case right after Joe had told Frank she was being promoted to lieutenant. Months before, Joe and Noah had kicked her ass to take the lieutenant's exam. She'd done it to get them off her back, and maybe because she didn't care, she'd scored in the top ten percent on both the written and oral tests. Joe had been pulling strings for almost a year but still only received the green light three weeks before his retirement. Frank had balked at advancement. She didn't want to command a squad. She just wanted to stay a Detective III, keep to herself, and drink away every last vestige of her past. But Joe and Noah wouldn't let her.

Swamped with all Joe had been trying to teach her before he left, Frank couldn't help her old partner. Noah had to work Pryce alone. The case was two months old and spilling into its second box by the time she took a look at it. Still overwhelmed by her new responsibilities, she hadn't offered much input. Noah actively worked the case for the better part of a year, chasing the tiniest of leads like a whippet after a mechanical rabbit. The rabbit always eluded him, but the boxes stayed by his desk.

Two years into her command, Frank noticed them by the cold files. After that, when his workload permitted, Noah would tackle the case again, always hoping he'd spot a lead he'd missed the first thirty dozen times. Frank had meant to help him with it—had started to a couple of times—but some crisis *du jour* always derailed her.

Frank's cigarette has burned down to her fingers. She takes a quick last suck on it then grinds it under her heel. She carries the musty boxes into her office. Pryce has just been reassigned.

Chapter 5

Frank takes a garment bag out of the closet. She lays it on the bed, unzips it and carefully removes her dress blues. She undresses in the adjoining bathroom and takes a long shower. She finds her blow-dryer under the sink and dries her hair. The smell of hot dust fills the room. She doesn't have the patience to finish her hair and leaves it damp against her neck.

Walking naked into the bedroom, she contemplates the clothes laid out on her bed. She never thought she'd have to wear them for this. Not for him.

She pins the gold bars on the collar. Satisfied they're straight, she slips into the heavy cloth. The shirt buttons snugly and Frank has to suck her breath in to zip her trousers. She tells herself she'd better spend more time on the treadmill. She pulls her dress belt through the pant loops and puts her tie on in front of the mirror. She doesn't look at her face.

Carrying her hat into the living room, she snaps her old .38 to the belt. She loves her 9mm, but today she feels a need to carry history. Creased and pressed, she drives alone to her best friend's funeral.

There, she stands with her squad, looking across the rectangle of plastic grass at Noah's family. Kennedy is there. Her old flame is subdued but solicitous. She asks why Gail didn't come.

"She wanted to. I asked her not to. Selfish of me, but this will be easier without her."

Frank has developed two personalities—a softer, more accessible personality reserved for rare intimates, and a professional, implacable police persona she uses to her advantage now. She braces herself, relieved when Kennedy doesn't press for detail. She's also relieved when Kennedy doesn't follow to the reception.

Cops and civilians make two separate knots, the former growing louder and raunchier as the liquor disappears. Joe Girardi is here. He's lost hair and gained weight. Frank doesn't know if she's glad to see him or not. She loves Joe, but his presence brings memories. Just like the old days, he pulls Frank away from the squad. She is both relieved and apprehensive.

"You look like you've been fucked, fried and flogged halfway to Friday."

It's such a classic Girardi line Frank has to smile.

Joe squeezes her shoulder, bending his head to hers. "How you doing, girlie-girl?"

"I'm okay."

"I know, I know. You're always okay. How you handling this?"

"Handling what?"

"Noah."

"I'm gonna figure out his caseload and his partner's—"

"No, no, no." Joe jabs a finger between her breasts. "How are *you* dealing with this?"

Frank stares over his shoulder. "Best I can. There's not a lot of options."

Joe stays quiet, but keeps his face in Frank's.

She manages a grin. "You're interrogating."

"Damn right." He grins back. "I know you won't give it up without a fight."

"Even then," she says, backing away, raising her palms in the air.

Joe shakes his head. "It'll eat you alive."

"I'll take care of it."

"How?"

"Joe, I respect you. Always have. But you're not my LT anymore. Don't push me."

"All right, all right," he soothes. "I'm just asking. I know what you're gonna do anyway."

"Oh, yeah? What's that?"

"You're gonna dive into a bottle and pretend it's never happened."

It rankles Frank that she is so transparent, and she answers, "So what if I do? Who's it gonna hurt?"

"You, girlie-girl. It's gonna hurt you. And it doesn't have to be that way."

"Maybe it does."

Frank stands squarely during Joe's full appraisal. She feels like she's let him down, but she can't change that. Finally he nods.

"Maybe it does. Come on," he says, swinging an arm around her neck. "Let's get back to the party."

He leaves soon after. Lightly slapping her cheek, Joe tells Frank to be careful. And reminds her she has his number. Watching him leave, she's surprised by the lump in her throat. She sips club soda so her crew can tie one on. As the funeral reception breaks up she pours them into cabs and sends them home with more sober revelers. She hugs Tracey and promises to call. She winds up alone in her car, driving with no destination. Like a serial killer, she cruises aimlessly until a perfect opportunity appears.

It's the Alibi. She locks her .38 into the lockbox in her trunk. In the bathroom she exchanges her uniform for shorts and a T-shirt from the backseat. They're wrinkled and stiff with sweat, but there's hardly anyone in the bar. Much of the Alibi's trade is from downtown offices so the place is quiet on Saturday afternoons. The weekend bartender doesn't know Frank well and tries to initiate conversation. When Frank shuts him down he takes up a position at the opposite end of the bar.

She stares at the NASCAR race over her head and drinks doubles. She did what she had to do at the wake, but now her time is her own, and she intends to use it getting shitfaced. As she finishes her third Scotch, Johnnie walks in. She doesn't admit how glad she is to see him. They order boilermakers and raise their shot glasses.

"To Noah."

They order again. By midnight they see two of themselves behind the jeweled bottles in the mirror. The bartender's afraid to cut the cops off and afraid not to. He's relieved when Frank tells him to call a cab. She and Johnnie tumble out to the sidewalk, Johnnie bellowing, "I'm drunker 'n a fuckin' lord!"

"Hella high," Frank agrees. She sways gently while Johnnie waggles a finger. Or two.

"La Freek." He calls her by the old nickname only he uses anymore. "You're drunker'n a fiddler's bitch."

"Uncanny, Detective Briggs. No foolin' you."

When the cab comes they go to another bar. By the time she gets home she has to kneel in front of her door and shut one eye to get the key in the lock. She gets in on the third try, stumbling past the flashing light on her answering machine. She knows who's called and it's too late to do anything about it. She drinks a big glass of water and takes four Excedrin PMs, hoping she'll sleep through the worst of the hangover.

It's a good plan, but at dawn Frank is hugging her john. After she's left with dry heaves she drinks more water and sticks her finger down her throat. When the water comes back up her stomach levels out. She chases two naproxen with an inch of Pepto Bismol and goes back to bed. The ringing phone wakes her. She reaches for it while assessing damage control. The hangover has left only a foggy head and sore stomach muscles.

21

"This is Franco."

"Hi." Gail's voice elicits remorse mingled with caution.

"Hey." Frank makes an offensive play. "I'm sorry I didn't call yesterday. Johnnie and I stopped by the Alibi and kind of closed the place down."

"Kind of closed the place down," Gail repeats, her words stuck in the wire like an icicle. "I don't suppose it ever occurred to you that I might be worried."

"Honestly, yes. But by the time I thought to call you I was pretty smashed."

While waiting for Gail's move Frank tries to remember how she got home. She walks to the living room window, doesn't see her car in the driveway and assumes she had sense enough to take a cab.

At last Gail says, "I hope you feel like bloody hell this morning."

"I do," Frank lies.

"Good. You deserve it."

The doc's honesty amuses Frank. It's what she loves most about Gail. That and her legs.

"I owe you dinner. How about I take you out and we catch a movie?"

"And you think that'll get you off the hook?"

"I don't know. Will it?"

Gail considers, allowing, "This time."

It's too late for Frank to go back to sleep so after a glass of chocolate milk she exorcises her guilt in the garage that is her gymnasium. With the Soloflex, treadmill and free weights, she sweats the night from her system. A cab takes her to the Alibi where her old Honda waits patiently. When she picks up Gail, she is bright-eyed and hungry. She will not drink tonight. She will be charming and attentive. Frank plans this, she thinks, to keep Gail off her back, to convince the doc everything is all right.

Chapter 6

Frank takes Lewis and Bobby aside after the Monday morning briefing. She asks them to clean out Noah's desk. It takes three boxes to hold all his gag toys, pictures, holiday decorations, art projects and birthday cards. Per her instructions, they leave the boxes in Frank's office. They are filled to the top, overflowing like Christmas stockings. She ignores them until the end of the day, when she walks across the street and comes back with two more boxes. She repacks everything until she can seal each box, thinking if it's this hard for her to look at his stuff, how hard is it going to be for his wife?

She calls Tracey, asking if she'd like company for dinner. She's pleased when Tracey answers, "Fuck, yeah. I'd love to see you."

Having six tender ears around hasn't bled the blue from Tracey's tongue.

Frank suggests, "How 'bout I get some Kentucky Fried Chicken? Wash it down with plastic coleslaw and watery potatoes?"

"God," Tracey groans. "I haven't eaten that shit in years. But the kids'll love it. And don't forget the biscuits and gravy."

When she arrives at Noah's house—it will always be Noah's house—Tracey greets her with the usual bear hug. What it lacks in exuberance it makes up for in comfort. The women hold on to each other for a while.

"Hey, I've got some stuff in the car. From Noah's desk. Want me to put it in the garage?"

"Would you?"

"Sure." Noah's youngest are watching TV in the living room and Frank says, "Hey, come help me bring your dinner in."

"Hi, Frank," Jamie says. "We're watching a movie."

"Not anymore," Tracey replies, waving the remote at the TV. "Go help Frank."

Frank loads the kids with bags of food, then stacks the boxes on a shelf in the garage. She brings a six-pack in from the car, but Tracey has already snapped the cap off a Bud and left it on the counter. Picking up her own bottle, she clanks it against Frank's.

She quips, "I was going to open a delicate little Pouilly-Fuissé but thought this might have a gutsier bouquet."

"Hear, hear," Frank says, draining much of her bottle in one go.

Tracey wipes her lip and says, "Thanks for coming by."

"Thanks for letting me invite myself."

"Well, hell, how can I refuse when you bring dinner?"

The kids aren't in the kitchen, so Frank asks, "How's it going?"

"Horrible. I can't stand this. Waiting for him to come into the room, or call and say he's running late. I don't know how many times a day I think, oh, I've gotta tell No this, and then each time it's a fresh kick in the stomach when I remember I can't." Tracey starts crying and yanks a paper towel off the holder. "I talk to him anyway. I like to think he can hear me, that he can still see us and knows how much we love him. What else can I do?" she pleads.

"Nothing."

"That's it." She nods. "Nothing. I cry all the time. My shirts are always wet," she jokes, but not really.

"It'll get better, Trace. You saw me go through Maggie. If I can do it, then anyone can."

"No kidding."

Tracey tries a chuckle, swiping her cheeks. Frank wraps her arms around her best friend's wife and for a minute they share the load.

The spring night is balmy, so they picnic on the patio. Tracey confides that they've been eating dinner everywhere except in the dining room. She can't stand seeing Noah's chair empty. After dinner, Tracey brings fresh beers. Leslie has disappeared into her room, but Mark and Jamie color near them.

Frank tilts her head, asking so they won't hear, "How are they?"

Tracey blows her sorrow and frustration out in a sigh. "Markie follows me everywhere I go, and at some point during the night Jamie joins us in bed. They're so confused. But at least they're talking about it. Les just hides in her room. She answers me in monosyllables but won't volunteer anything."

"It's harder for some people."

"I guess."

Frank lets Tracey study her.

"I was always amazed how you just sat and drank. You never said a word about Maggie. I used to push No to get you to talk but he'd just tell me to butt out. He said you would if you wanted to. Did you? Ever?"

Frank squints into the past. "Couple times. When I was drunk enough."

For almost a month after her lover had been killed Frank would come over and pass out on the Jantzens' couch. Noah would stay up with her until she fell asleep. The poor bastard had almost died trying to match her drink for drink and Tracey finally made him stop. But still he'd stayed up with Frank. They talked about little things, work and news. They shared silences interrupted only by the gurgle of Frank's bottle.

Frank asks, "You remember the Pryce case?"

"Do I? Christ Almighty, Noah lived that case. He ate, drank and breathed it. Why? Did you get a bite on it?"

Frank's head shakes in the negative. "I was thinking about taking a look at it."

"Good luck," Tracey says. "Excuse me, but I hated those fucking kids. Noah'd obsess about them all day at work, then when he finally came home he'd go straight upstairs to watch the kids sleep. He'd fall asleep on the floor and I finally stopped waking him up. I'd just cover him with a blanket and leave him there. That's where I found him Christmas morning. He stuck around long enough to open presents then he spent the rest of the day at work. He stayed with his kids all night then went back to those goddamned dead ones in the morning." Tracey shivers. "I hated that case."

"Kid cases are tough. Worse for people with their own. Joe knew he was taking it hard, but he said every cop's got to go through it. That it'd either make him or break him."

"Yeah, well, it almost broke him. And then when the evidence came up missing? Christ, Frank, I honestly thought he was going to kill somebody. I'd never seen him that angry."

"I remember."

Most of the physical evidence in the Pryce case had been lost after analysis at the Scientific Investigation Division. Noah had gone on a rampage and practically instigated a lawsuit against SID.

Frank grins. "I don't think I've ever seen him any madder. The SID techs wouldn't work his cases for months afterwards. Said they'd only work with me or his partner."

"That's right. You'd just gotten promoted." After a pause in which Frank again reflects on how she wasn't there for Noah, Tracey says, "It was good to see Joe, wasn't it?"

"Yeah. Glad he came."

"I assume you're the one who told him?"

Frank nods. The beer is mildly anesthetic. Because she fears undoing its tender effects, she focuses on someone else's pain. "How are No's folks?"

"I don't know. His mom still can't talk on the phone, and Larry, well, Larry's Larry. 'Fine, fine, all right. Everything's just fine. Awful business, but we'll get through.' He's got that whole Leslie Howard, stiff-upper-lip thing going on. But he's right. We'll muddle through somehow, huh?"

Stretching for Tracey's hand, Frank squeezes it tight. She see herself begowned and turbaned. She has become Stoic the Magnificent, the Great Bearer of Lies sweet to the ear and a balm to the heart.

"That's right," she assures. "We will."

Chapter 7

Cases are redistributed, detective teams are rearranged, and work at the nine-three proceeds over the next few weeks, albeit haltingly at times, without Noah Jantzen. The cluckhead who suffocated her baby was turned in, although not from altruism, as Frank predicted. The junkie's sister is a cluckhead too and rats her out to Lewis for a twenty. Bobby and Darcy catch a domestic grounder and close a corner slice-and-dice. Foubarelle throws make-work at Frank while hounding her for stats. It's all s-squared, d-squared—same shit, different day.

The Pryce murder books perch on a corner of Frank's desk. She's stared at them without the guts to open them. They seem like they're still Noah's. This case is the last she has of him. She doesn't want to pore over the binders without him peering over her shoulder.

What if he is, she thinks. Tracey likes to think so. The idea embarrasses Frank. Not so much because it's ludicrous, but because she finds an edge of comfort in it.

The day is over. Only Frank and Darcy remain upstairs in Homicide. Darcy types outside her office and the tap-tap of his keystrokes is reassuring. Frank chides her superstition, but the admonishment is halfhearted. Since the day that Darcy inexplicably saved Frank's neck from a crazed Santerist's knife, she is willing to allow that things may exist 'twixt heaven and earth which she can't explain with only five senses.

She arranges papers and folders to one side of the desk, clearing a space to work in. Then she puts one of the Pryce binders in the empty spot and pulls her wooden chair close. She takes the crime scene pictures out and sorts them to reflect how the responding officer and subsequent personnel would have approached the scene. She studies the first picture for a long time.

It is a wide-angle color shot taken from the street. The bottom foreground includes a sidewalk spilling over into a weedy, garbage-strewn lot. A house lies in a charred pile in the center of the lot, the rubble having been heavily scavenged over time. Gutted, overstuffed furniture and rusted appliances dot the property. Plastic sacks and potato chip bags hang like flags from weed poles.

The lot is delineated on the left by a house with plank and corrugated fencing. Dead banana leaves drape over the fence at the rear of the lot. A plywood fence starts at the left rear corner and continues to the right rear corner of the lot. Along the right side of the lot, a four-foot chain link encircles a neatly kept house. Roofs are visible behind the houses and the plywood fence. All the roofs are roughly the same height. Three windows in the house on the right overlook the lot.

The next picture is a close-up of the ruined house. A handful of moldered sheetrock panels affixed to blackened 2 x 4s suggest the building's basic structure. Rubble and tall weeds obscure the interior. She scrutinizes the flotsam and jetsam. Nothing jumps out as extraordinary.

She flips to a new photo. Taken from the right side of the house, it looks into the shell of a large room. The skeletal framing suggests the photographer is shooting into what was the living room. Differently-sized footprints stand out against a concrete foundation overlaid with detritus from junkies, trannies, kids and taggers.

Almost unnoticed among the clutter, two heads jut from a dull green blanket spread on the right side of the room. Ashy faces jut toward the camera. Frank wants to see more, but aware of the luxury of time, she patiently resurveys the presented debris. Broken glass, twisted rebar, water-warped papers, a busted lawn chair, bottle caps, fresh candy wrappers, age-silvered cigarette packs—nothing in the litter seems unusual. She doesn't see it in this picture, but she is sure the trash obscures condoms, syringes and fading skin mags.

But that's speculation, which comes later. Right now Frank wants to see the scene as if she's walking into it for the first time. The first inconsistency she sees is the garbage splaying from under the carefully covered bodies. If the perp was thoughtful enough to arrange the kids side by side and cover them with a blanket, why didn't he clear away the garbage first? Frank puts the question to paper, studying the photo a few minutes more. When she places it facedown, a fresh one stares from the stack.

Two black children lie next to each other, on their backs, eyes closed, covered to their chins with the blanket. Their mouths are wrapped with duct tape. Above the tape, patches on the right side of the boy's face appear blanched, as if he were cheek-down while his blood settled. The girl's hair twists out from a barrette in wild tufts. The boy's skull is shaved close, but his head is oddly bent. Frank studies the girl's neck where there are marks in the flesh. She'll see close-ups of the marks in the autopsy photos.

The blanket is army-issue green. Not torn or stained, though slightly smudged with what looks like dust. Frank thinks the perp brought it with him. Because men kill more often than women, Frank will stick with the masculine pronoun, but she will not exclude the possibility that the offender is female.

Frank draws a line down a sheet of legal paper. On the left she lists ideas, on the right, supporting facts:

Dump job, killed elsewhere	*Garbage not displaced/no mud, debris in hair*
Perp brought blanket	*Blanket's clean*
Perp knew kids/ feels remorse	*Spontaneity of attack/took time to cover them, arrange them*
Perp lives nearby/not mobile? Wants them to be found? (Remorse again) /no alternate disposal options?	*Kids carefully positioned but left in garbage*

Frank has more thoughts but decides to wait until she's seen the rest of the pictures before committing them to paper.

The next shot is tighter, closer to the bodies, and the blanket has been removed. The boy is smaller than the girl, who's between nine and twelve, Frank thinks. She knows her age but has forgotten and doesn't want to remember. The boy looks to be from five to seven. The girl is thin and gangly, but the boy still carries his baby fat. He appears fully clothed, in blue jeans, sneakers and a plain blue windbreaker. Under the jacket he wears a red sweatshirt. A white T-shirt pokes from beneath the sweatshirt, and white socks cover his ankles.

The girl wears a mustard-yellow sweater over a pink blouse, a sky-blue skirt, pink socks and one sneaker. Her arms and legs are straight. Postmortem lividity darkens the posterior edges of her thighs and calves. There appear to be smudges on her legs but the girl's clothes and skin are relatively clean. Frank thinks the kids were carried, not dragged.

She adds the last fact to the column opposite where she's written dump job. She also adds that the offender is likely male because the victims were carried to the site. A woman could have brought them, but she'd have to be pretty strong to pick her way through the rubble, probably in the dark, carrying at least a fifty-pound load each, more if the kids were carried together.

On the sheet underneath, Frank writes these reminders:

31

Sneaker? panties?

Blood on site, perp tripped (cut himself)?

Frank is fairly sure there is no blood, but she'll double-check. She also thinks the other sneaker was found on the lot. The panties are a different story.

She examines the tape covering their mouths. It appears to be standard duct tape. Interestingly, and this could be a significant MO if this perp has committed similar assaults, the tape is wrapped at least twice around their heads, maybe three times. She looks at the boy's wrists. They are bound in front of him and wrapped at least twice around, as are his calves. The perp's thorough. The visible ends of tape are neatly torn, not cut. She thinks the perp is used to working with his hands.

The girl is bound only around the mouth. He must have felt he had control of her. Frank feels herself slipping into the perp's skin. It's like sinking her feet into sticky, sulphurous mud—not a completely unpleasant experience if one accepts the mud for what it is. Frank is willing to sink further, but not now.

First she has to court her suspect, woo him to her. She can initiate foreplay once she has assembled the facts about him. The climax of their union comes when she walks through her reconstructed scenario as the perp, when she *is* the perp, feeling what he felt, doing what he did and thinking like he thought. Ninety-eight percent of the cases landing on her desk are unsuitable for this level of involvement and Frank regrets she doesn't have the opportunity to profile more often. She's often dallied with the notion of applying to the FBI's Behavioral Science Unit where she could profile full-time. She meets all the criteria—an older individual with extensive time in service; objective; analytical; can think like a perp; practical . . .

Aware that she has strayed from the case, she is pleased anew with the luxury of being able to do so. Though she has time to kill, Frank's habit, training and tacit need to immerse herself in a life other than her own sends her back to the pictures.

She taps Ladeenia Pryce with a forefinger. She's the case. Clothed and secured, the boy is inconsequential. The perp focused his energy on the girl. Frank is so immersed in the photograph she doesn't notice Darcy standing in the doorway. She jumps when he growls, "Good night."

"Jesus," she breathes.

"No, just me," he says, a thin grin under his moustache.

The clock over her door reads six-thirty and Frank says, "You put in a long day."

Darcy shrugs under a leather jacket. "They're all long."

"Roger that," Frank says. She almost offers to buy him a cup of coffee. If he drank, she'd offer beers at the Sizzler, but she withdraws the invitation even before it's issued. Darcy gets his reports in on time, can handle himself on the street and works well with Bobby, but he keeps his distance from the squad. Frank respects his privacy and doesn't want to put him in the awkward position of refusing his boss. Instead she asks, "How's Gabby?"

His daughter has cystic fibrosis and lives with her mother in Orange County.

"Not so good. She was in the hospital Sunday night."

Frank thinks back. "But you were here Monday."

"She was out by ten. We took her back to Margarite's and I stayed until she fell asleep."

"Darcy, take the time if you need it."

"Oh, I will," he vows. "Believe me."

Frank nods. "See you tomorrow."

Darcy lifts his Harley helmet and she listens to him leave. She'd told Gail she'd make dinner tonight, but now that she's started on the Pryce case she'd like to get through the photographs in one sitting. Plus, Frank has been living on doughnuts and Del Taco burritos. She has no interest in cooking or eating. But drinking's another story.

Frank tries Gail's office with no luck. She dials Gail's home number and leaves a message, then leaves the same message on her cell phone—that she has to work and will be home later, sorry about dinner. Gail will probably be disappointed but not surprised. Activities planned around a homicide lieutenant's and chief coroner's schedules are always hopeful and rarely realized.

Frank is about to return to the photographs but thinks better of it. Eyeing the wall clock, she decides if she wants that drink, she'd better get it now. Gail will forgive Frank for working late, but not for stopping at the Alibi. Tucking the photos under a binder cover, Frank cradles the Pryce books under her arm like a newly sprouted appendage.

Chapter 8

Alone in a booth, Frank retrieves her stack of photographs. She gulps a double while looking at additional scene shots. From a different angle, she sees there is a mattress only a few feet from the bodies.

Wondering why the perp didn't put them there, she's again struck by the incongruity of the tenderness with which the kids were placed on a garbage pile. She surmises it is dark when he dumps the bodies, and though he may be familiar with the lot's location, he's not intimate with the interior. He doesn't know the mattress is there.

Boards, flattened boxes and sections of large appliances wedged between the remaining 2x4s create partial walls. The pseudo walls are covered inside and out with tags, taunts and warnings to stay out. Frank particularly likes TRESPASERS WILL BE SMOKT. Because the graffiti is amateurish and lacks authority, she thinks wannabe bangers with no established ties are using the gutted site as a hangout.

She writes this down even though the Pryce case doesn't appear gang-related. With a fresher case she might not bother with least likely scenarios, but on this one she has nothing to lose. On the contrary, eliminating as many possibilities as she can will narrow her search field of suspects.

Delivering Frank's second drink, the waitress warns, "Okay. Time to order dinner."

Frank has promised Nancy she'll eat after her first drink. Frank settles on a BLT and Nancy is satisfied. She's made a career of fussing over Frank.

Finished for the time being with the crime scene, Frank starts on the autopsy reports. Trevor Pryce is a normally developed six-year-old boy. He has numerous scrapes, scabs and contusions but none relative to his cause of death, which the reporting coroner listed as gross disarticulation at the first and second cervical discs. Torn ligaments and spiral fractures indicate the boy's head was twisted until his neck snapped.

Nancy brings Frank's sandwich, returning a moment later with a Coke. Frank would rather have a beer but doesn't want Gail to smell it on her. She picks at her French fries while searching the document for an entry that might indicate signs of a struggle or fall. There's nothing—no evidence of assault, no cranial laceration or contusions, no twist fractures. Just a broken neck.

Scandalous, Frank mocks. She tackles her sandwich, refusing to engage this case with anything other than professional interest. While she is actually admiring a perp with the grapes to kill so intimately and dispassionately, it nags her that his MO so completely contradicts how he left the bodies.

The girl's autopsy report adds to this discrepancy, reinforcing that Ladeenia Pryce is the focus of the murders. Her child's body shows further inconsistencies—a fresh, half-inch burn on the outside of her right thumb, a swollen, rounded contusion on her right breast, horizontal stripes indented on the back of her left thigh. Frank finds the close-up of the leg markings. The edges of the impression are blurry, but it is clearly composed of straight, parallel lines. She concentrates on the pattern but it remains indecipherable.

Frank squints at what could be bruises mottling the girl's arms. Where the skin has blanched on the back of the arms, the bruising is more vivid. A couple contusions dot her legs. They all appear fresh. The ME cited cause of death as asphyxia resulting from manual strangulation, and Frank studies the telltale choke marks circling her neck. The bruising is too indistinct to determine if the perp choked her from the front or the rear. Frank finishes her sandwich while reading clinical descriptions of brutal vaginal and anal assaults.

Deciding to risk Gail's wrath, she signals for one more double, then bends her head back over the autopsy pictures. Lividity in the girl is pronounced posteriorly. The skin on the back of her torso and extremities is pale where contact pressure excluded the settling blood, yet the photos indicate anterior blanching on her torso as well. Her face and anterior extremities are unblanched. Frank checks the boy's lividity. His is completely anterior.

A picture forms in Frank's mind and she quickly commits it to paper. Noah, Gail, even her drink is forgotten as Frank immerses herself into the world of Ladeenia and Trevor Pryce. She will be a long time leaving them.

Chapter 9

When Frank walks into Gail's apartment, Gail swivels from her computer and removes her glasses. She says hello and offers her lips to Frank. Frank kisses her cheek, calculating how soon she can get back to her murder books.

"What came up?" Gail asks.

"A cold case, actually."

"You stood me up for a cold case?"

"It's not just any case. It's one Noah's been working on for years. I've been meaning to get to it and finally opened it this afternoon. Once I started looking I got on a roll and couldn't stop. I needed to see it all at once, just like a fresh scene."

Gail bites her lower lip.

"It's important," Frank insists. "A brother and a sister, six and nine. Jamie and Leslie were about six when Noah caught the case. It hit him hard. I'd just gotten promoted and couldn't help him with it." Frank hefts a shoulder.

"I see. So you're helping him now."

"Something like that."

"Isn't that kind of like closing the barn door after the horse is out?"

"Meaning what?"

"Never mind."

Gail turns back to the computer screen, but Frank justifies, "It's still an open case. The parents moved up the coast but No still keeps in contact with them . . ." She trails off, realizing her mistake. "He worked it off and on when he could, but he couldn't get anywhere with it. Maybe I can see it with fresh eyes. See something he couldn't. In fact, would you look at this for me?"

Frank digs through her briefcase, producing an anterior autopsy photo of Ladeenia Pryce's body.

"Look at this blanching. My first thought was she'd been moved before lividity set, but see how it's only on the torso and a little on the upper thighs?"

Despite her indifference, professional curiosity makes Gail peek at the photo.

Frank explains, "I'm thinking she was on her back but that there was something on top of her. A weight that caused the anterior blanching, because look at this." Replacing the picture with a close-up, she points to the extensive pallor along the girl's backside. "Do you think that could account for such a pattern?"

"It could."

She shows Gail another photograph. "This is the brother. I'm thinking the perp put him on top of her. Laid them face to face. See the blanching on her chest? And on her hip and thigh? Maybe that's where his legs draped over hers. Think that'd fit?"

Looking more closely at Frank now than the picture, Gail says, "Sure."

She turns back to her computer and Frank packs up the photographs. She heads to the kitchen for a beer. Sipping it at the sink, deciding what to do with the rest of the night, she's surprised when Gail joins her.

"Baby, I know this is a hard time for you. And it's hard watching you go through this. I wish there was something I could do, but I can't. I feel like most of the time you don't even want me around. I know you've got to do your own thing, but I hate being so completely shut out."

"You're not shut out. I'm here, aren't I?"

"Are you?"

Because Frank doesn't like the answer to that question she takes an offensive tack. "Look. I'm sorry I'm not dealing with this the way you'd like me to. Maybe—"

"Oh, don't you *dare* put this on me, Frank. Don't even think about it. How you deal with this is your business and I'm trying to give you the latitude to do that, but you've got to understand how frustrating it is watching you cope by drinking and working to excess. We don't talk about anything more significant than the weather, and when I push for something more you get sarcastic and combative. I'm trying to be patient, but I don't feel like you're making any effort to deal with this."

Frank clamps her jaws together. Her fingers whiten around the bottle but Frank is contained. "Let me see if I understand this. I'm the one who goes to work in the building I've shared with him for fourteen years. I'm the one who passes his empty desk every day. I'm the one who spends half my time thinking of things I have to tell him, and the other half remembering I can't. I'm the one who's there for his fucking widow and his fucking kids, but I'm not making any effort to *deal* with it? Did I get that right?"

Gail argues, "Staring down his memory is not the same as grieving him. You're ignoring your feelings around Noah just like you ignored Maggie. You can't brush this all under the carpet and expect it to disappear. Didn't you learn anything sitting in Clay's office? You have to talk about these things, Frank. You have to *feel* them to make them go away, not just bury them under piles of empties!"

Frank shouts back, "I don't want to feel anything, Gail. Get it? And I don't want to talk about it. I'm not indulging in all this namby-pamby, touchy-feely, get-it-all-out-on-the-table bullshit. Not right now. And the bottom line is, all that Doctor Phil shit just gets you a bigger heartache. It's a waste of fucking time. I will deal with this in my own way, in my own time, and it if you can't handle that, then I will be more than happy to stay the fuck away."

With marvelous restraint Frank tips her bottle into the sink and stalks to the front door. Gail follows.

"Oh, let me guess! This is the part where you storm out like you always do when we argue. Why don't you stay and finish this? Just this one time."

"It's finished."

"No, it's not. You're just running from me, too. When are you going to *face* life, Frank? You can't take off like a big bird every time we have a fight. For such a big, tough cop you have a remarkably wide yellow streak."

"Oh, nice," Frank throws over her shoulder. "Now we've resorted to name-calling."

"If the shoe fits . . ."

Wheeling, Frank demands, "Gail, why are you making a hard situation even harder? What the hell do you want from me? Blood?"

"I want *you*. The real you. Not this cold, awful shell you've become. I want the Frank who laughs and talks and hurts and yes, bleeds. The real Frank. Not this morose, withdrawn carcass you drag home every night."

"Maybe that's all I can give you right now."

Frank watches Gail make the effort to say, "Okay. I know that. I just miss the real Frank. I get impatient waiting for her to come back. I miss her."

Frank fixes her eyes on Gail's, considering her options. Gail's probably right. She usually is about this sort of thing. Frank knows

41

her emotions are overriding her intellect and she despises her lack of control. She can swallow her pride and let go of the argument, or stay mad and justify her stance. But Frank is too tired to stay mad. Her fight drains away and she concedes, "It might be a while, Gay."

"I know. You're going to do it your way. It's just so frustrating not being able to help."

Frank understands. She feels that way with Tracey, wishing she could carry the hurt for her. For the kids, too. Gail holds her arms open and Frank steps into them. Into the doc's hair, she murmurs, "Been a long day. What say we hit the hay?"

And though Frank sleeps close to Gail, she remains distant.

Chapter 10

Her office door is closed and the knock surprises her. She weighs the sound of the appeal and guesses Jill is on the other side.

"Yeah?"

The red-haired detective pops her head in. "Is this a bad time?"

"No. Come in."

Frank watches Jill approach her desk. She seems hesitant. Lifting a handful of papers she says, "The sixty-day on Fuentes."

"Fuentes?"

"The domestic battery? We're trying to find her boyfriend?"

"Right." Frank remembers. She glances through Jill's late report, asks a couple questions. They discuss another case and the comp time Jill wants to take. "Anything else?" Frank asks.

Jill's hesitancy returns. She's an opinionated, determined woman and this timidity is intriguing.

"Spit it out," Frank encourages.

"Well, um, we were just, I mean *I* was, wondering, how, um, how you're doing and stuff. We know, I know, how close you were to No and it's, well, it's not easy."

Jesus, Frank explodes in her head, *won't anyone give this a fucking rest?* Lacing her fingers in front of her mouth, she rests her chin in her thumbs, surmising, "So the boys sent you in to do the dirty work."

"We're just worried, is all."

"What's the consensus out there?"

"What consensus?"

"Do you think I'm gonna go postal and spray the squad room with a shotgun, or just eat my gun and make a helluva mess on the bedroom wall?"

"Nobody thinks that," Jill flares, her timidity vanishing. "It's just that you haven't been on any of the call-outs lately. That's not like you. And your door's closed all the time and you barely talk to anyone, except at brief. We're just concerned."

"Well, you don't need to be. All you need to do—and you can pass this on to the boys—is mind your own business and do your jobs. If you spent more time worrying about your sixty-days than me, you might be able to get them in on time."

Jill's lips purse up and she glares.

"Anything else?" Frank repeats.

Jill shakes her head, slamming Frank's door when she leaves.

"Christ, what a cabal," Frank speaks into her fingers. Talking to herself is another recently acquired habit that Frank's beginning to notice.

She leans back with a rushing sigh, wishing everyone would disappear into a black hole and take their goddamned concern with them. She knows Jill meant well, and knows she shouldn't have shot the messenger. She'll admit things have changed around the squad room. She seems to have closed her door literally as well as metaphorically and can't get it open again. Isn't even trying. She doesn't care that she's locked it behind her and she wishes no one else did either.

And again her temper's gotten the better of her. Now she'll have to apologize to Jill, make nice to the squad. Frank's job is to maintain morale even though her own is lower than piss in a gutter. She sighs again, unable to get enough air.

Frank pulls herself out of her chair. Jill is on the phone. Frank lays a hand on her shoulder, points to her office. Jill nods and joins her a few minutes later.

"Do you want the door open or closed?"

"Open. Sit down." She waits until her detective is perched on the vinyl office chair. "Jill, I'm sorry. I shouldn't have snapped at you. I guess I'm not dealing with this the way everybody would like me to. But I *am* dealing with it. And you're right. It is hard. But I don't want you guys worrying. If you have concerns about the way I'm running things, tell me. I'll listen. It's just going to take some time to readjust, that's all. We've taken a lot of punches lately, but we'll bounce back. We always do, right?"

There she is, Stoic the Magnificent again.

"Yeah," Jill agrees. "It's just that we care a—"

"Look. I know," Frank interrupts. "But don't worry. That's my job. Everything's gonna be okay."

Jill nods and Frank dismisses her gently. She returns to the work on her desk, satisfied she's extinguished another fire. Frank's been pushing so much of it lately she's starting to believe her own hype.

Chapter 11

Something else the squad's probably noticed—after having spent her career practically living at Figueroa, Frank's been leaving the station promptly at quitting time. Too many ghosts wander the halls. Nor does she want to be at Gail's. There she has to pretend too hard. Pretend everything's okay, pretend she's fine. She is, of course, just not the way Gail and anyone else with half an opinion would like her to be.

Her house is empty and it echoes, but there at least Frank can spread the Pryce case across the dining room table and get lost in their world. Grim as it is, she prefers it to her own. She likes long stretches of time with the case and a full bottle of Black Label. Even on the nights she has to go to Gail's, if she leaves at two and traffic is fair, she can manage a solid four or five hours on the case.

Frank's tired at end-of-watch today; too tired to think well, but drink in hand she reaches for the binders anyway.

"Light reading," she tells herself.

Ladeenia Pryce was killed on her way to a friend's house. The friend, Cassie Bertram, lived in a duplex three blocks away. She never got to Cassie's house. Her friend called Mrs. Pryce to ask when Ladeenia was coming. Mrs. Pryce told Cassie that Ladeenia had already left. And Trevor went with her. Mrs. Pryce told Cassie to have Ladeenia turn around and come right home when she did get there—Ladeenia had fooled around getting over there and now it was almost suppertime. That was at 4:30 PM.

At 5:30, Mrs. Pryce called Cassie to tell her daughter to get her butt home, but Ladeenia still hadn't arrived at her friend's house. That was when Mrs. Pryce started to get scared. Ladeenia was a good girl. Her daddy spoiled her a little but she minded well. Mrs. Pryce hoped she'd been sidetracked by another friend. Maybe that little Guatemalan girl that lived down Gage, or some children at the playground. Ladeenia was a friendly girl, and responsible. She took good care of Trevor. She wouldn't do anything foolish if he was with her.

Mrs. Pryce planned on giving Ladeenia a good hiding when she got home. Teach that girl to tell her mama where she was and to be home when she was supposed to be. By 8:30, Mrs. Pryce was panicking. Her husband called the Figueroa station. Adults and older teens had to have been gone for at least twenty-four hours before they were officially considered missing. It was different for a six- and nine-year-old in the middle of winter, four hours after sundown. The desk sergeant told Mr. Pryce to come down and file a report. He did so and his description of the kids was read at the next roll call. Not that it mattered. The autopsy reports would later conclude that Ladeenia and Trevor were dead by then.

At 1:12 the following afternoon a hysterical woman called the station. One of her laying hens had come up missing and she'd been searching the nearby vacant lot. She didn't find her chicken, but she did find Ladeenia and Trevor.

The suits were called, and just the luck of the draw, Frank and

Noah were up. But Frank was in Ventura, stuck in a weekend empowerment seminar, so Noah fielded the call alone. He didn't leave the scene until well after dark, long after the coroner's wagon had taken the bodies away, long after the SID techs had finished bagging and tagging, long after every last picture had been snapped and every diagram sketched. Noah had walked into the darkened squad room as Frank was walking out. They'd turned the lights on and she sat and listened to him, promising to help as soon as she could. "As soon as she could" wasn't soon enough and Noah worked the case alone.

Frank reads Noah's interviews with Mr. and Mrs. Pryce. She reads the interviews with their other children. While she reads an interview with one of Ladeenia's friends, Frank refills her tumbler. She drinks and reads, making occasional notes until the alarm on her watch tells her it's time to go to Gail's. A stone sinks in her chest. With effort, she closes the binder.

Chapter 12

A contentious lieutenant's meeting on Thursday goes well past dinnertime. Frank returns to the office for her things. The squad room is quiet, her cops long gone. It's not so bad at night. Not so many memories, no interruptions. Frank finds the stale Camels in her desk drawer. She fires one up and sinks into her chair. The smoke makes her dizzy but she drags it in anyway. She savors the weight in her chest. It displaces all the other ones. She spits tobacco off her lip and when the cigarette burns to within a half an inch of her fingers, she pinches it out between thumb and forefinger. It's a residual reflex from a two-pack-a-day habit. Now it hurts like hell because she has no calluses. Frank smells burnt skin and a fleeting, rigored grin slices her face.

If she could see herself in a mirror, she might see glimpses of the scum she's spent a lifetime trying to put away: the fourteen-year-old who raped his grandmother with a serving spoon; the father who admitted to daily intercourse with his four- and six-year-olds because that's what he had kids for; the mother who giggled when she shocked her infant with a stripped electrical cord then beat the baby because it cried; the old man who suffocated his wife of fifty-two years because he was tired of wiping her bedridden ass and changing her soiled sheets; the ten-year-old who shot her grandmother because she wouldn't let her stay up to watch *Survivor*.

But there's no mirror in the room. Frank lights another cigarette, carrying on with the illusion that she's human. She sucks smoke in and mouths it toward the ceiling in fat doughnuts. She feels nothing. Absolutely nothing, and that's the way she wants it.

The Pryce kids whisper to her like smack whispers to a junkie. Frank swings her feet to the floor and opens the thick books. She spends her night in the mind of a man who binds a boy's wrists, hands and mouth with duct tape, them makes him watch and listen while he rapes the boy's sister, front and back, then chokes her to death. Frank spends her night in the head of a man like that and feels nothing.

It's almost one in the morning before she thinks to look at a clock. She crashes on the couch and is thickheaded the next day. She leaves work promptly at two. At home, she changes into shorts and starts working out. She's contemplating dinner, and a couple beers, when Bobby calls.

"We got a kid shot while he was waiting for the bus, and there are reporters everywhere."

"Sure there are. Kids get shot in South Central every day but this one's a story because it's four o'clock on a slow news day. I'll be there as soon I can."

Frank hangs up and gets back into the suit she took off less than an hour ago. She repacks her pockets and belt. The holster gets cinched back under her arm.

"Christ, I do not need this," she mutters, slamming the front door behind her.

Traffic is excruciating and she bangs the dashboard, more in time with frustration than the hip-hop booming from her abused speakers. News vans and police cars are still clogging the scene when she arrives. The paramedics are long gone, but the coroner's people have beaten her to the site. It's a routine cap and they've already released the body. An SID technician is collecting a through-and-through in a scrawl of blood beside the boy. A man weeps behind the tape, encircled by anguished faces trying to comfort him. His nightmare is just beginning, but for Frank the scene is comfortably routine.

"S'up?" she asks Darcy.

"Sixteen-year-old black male. Vic's name is Clyde Payson. He was waiting for the bus with his friends when a male black approached him. They started arguing, got into a fight, and the suspect fired on him. A forty-four. The friends recognized the shooter. Harlan Miller."

"Sweet. Let's get this wrapped with a ribbon. Early Christmas present for the chief, and it'll get these bastards"—she tosses her head at the reporters—"off our backs. Who's the guy crying over there?"

"The kid's father. He was a couple blocks away at the car wash."

"Talk to him yet?"

"Not too much. He usually gives the kid a ride home from school, but he and his friends were taking the bus to the mall."

"Affiliation?"

When Darcy shakes his head, Frank realizes how long his hair is.

"Doesn't appear to be a banger."

"Darcy, am I your fucking mother? Can't you get ever get a haircut without me telling you to?"

Darcy stares at Frank. Then he spits tobacco just far enough from Frank's feet to keep it from splattering on her very expensive shoes. He's not supposed to be chewing at a crime scene.

"Sure," he answers without taking his eyes from hers.

Frank wants to bitch-slap him but has sense enough to know she's already stepped out of line. She also knows her team's been carrying her lately. And because they're good at what they do, she usually cuts them slack. Her job is to field the heat from upstairs so her detectives

51

can do their job, not ride them about chickenshit details like haircuts and chew.

"Jesus on a fucking pony," she relents. "What about the suspect? Does he claim?"

"Rollin' Forties."

"Okay, what else?"

"According to the kid's friends, the shooter's seventeen. Goes to school at Crenshaw, lives near there."

"Okay."

Frank nods and steps to the tape. She gives the reporters a brief rundown, withholding specifics about the shooter and ending with the assurance that there will be more details issued from the Media Relations Section. Done with that, she tracks down the rest of the nine-three squad and calls them in. Lewis and Diego are assigned to run Miller through the databases. Johnnie and Jill help Darcy and Bobby collect statements while memories are fresh.

At 8:00 PM, Frank and her two primaries sit in Clyde Payson's living room. His family is gathered around. They can't understand this. Clyde is a straight-A student at Crenshaw High. He's already prepping to get into UCLA, where his mother went. He's not a banger. He's a star on the basketball team. He wants to play for the NBA. He has a cell phone and uses it to let his parents know where he is, what he's doing and when he'll be home. He was just going to the mall to get new clothes for a trip to Georgia. The family is leaving in less than a week to visit relatives Clyde's never met. He and his youngest sister haven't flown before and can't wait to get on the plane. Now Clyde's on a refrigerated tray in the coroner's office. The family's going to a funeral instead of Atlanta. They did everything right. They don't understand why Clyde was killed.

Frank's been doing this almost twenty years and still doesn't understand. She knows the family never will either. Sense can't be made of the nonsensical. Like a triage surgeon, all she can do is stem the blood flow, one suspect at a time. Frank and her crew work through the night and into the morning. Harlan Miller is in the wind but Payson's murder snaps the community from its apathy.

Almost twenty-four hours after Clyde Payson is gunned down, an anonymous caller drops a dime on Miller, a.k.a. BKilla. The tipster says he's at the home of another Rollin' 40s member. Frank organizes backup and they converge on an apartment complex in Crip turf. They bust in on a startled Miller and two homes dripping forty-ouncers at a kitchen table. The three of them scatter like roaches under a light. Given their positions when they walked in, Frank is the first to peel after Miller. Gun drawn, she chases him down a hall into a shaded bedroom. Miller is crawling halfway through a window and Frank yanks him back by his waistband. He thrashes against the windowsill. Afraid she'll lose him if he slips out of his pants, she holsters the Beretta and wrestles him back through the window. Bobby and Darcy catch up and grab Miller on either side. Panting, Frank lets her boys have him. Miller curses and struggles as they cuff him. While the detectives are catching their breath, he hawks a spitball at Frank. It lands on her leg.

"Oh, that wasn't nice," she says, pulling her trouser leg away from her shin and examining the wad. "Or smart. That's assaulting an officer, you crab asshole."

"Kiss my blue Crip ass," he challenges. Then adds, "Bulldyke bitch."

"Oh-h-h. That wasn't smart either," Frank says.

"Whachu gonna do?" he snarls, dancing from foot to foot. "Hit me? Pull out your big sticks and beat on me?"

"Don't tempt me," Frank says. "Let's go."

She starts to clear a path through a cluster of women who have gathered in the bedroom. They chatter like magpies for the cops to leave their house, and Miller calls over their angry voices, "Suck my Crip dick, fucking five-oh cunt."

Frank hears the commotion and turns in time to see Darcy shove Miller against the wall. She should have turned around and kept walking out of the room. Instead she joins Darcy. Flapping a hand at the women, she tells Bobby, "Get 'em outta here."

"Aw, come on, Frank. Let's just go."

She whirls on Bobby, ordering. "I said get 'em out!"

Her vehemence surprises him as much as it does her. Frank is stepping over a line and knows it, but it feels too good to stop. She's a runaway train gathering steam. Crossing the room, she plants herself in front of Miller.

"Uncuff him," she tells Darcy.

Darcy does, grinning. Miller rubs his wrists.

"Hey, punk-ass bitch. You got something to say to me? Hm? I can't hear you." When he is silent she smirks. "Not so mouthy now, are you?"

He spits over his shoulder, mumbling into it.

Frank glances around the room. Seeing Bobby's cleared it, she steps into Miller's face. "If you're gonna say something, be man enough to say it loud enough so I can hear. Or ain't you got the balls?"

"I got 'em," he says, hefting his crotch. "Right here. More than your dyke ass can handle."

"That's right," Frank agrees. "You're too much man for me. That's why I had to get wit' your baby sister last night. You know she shaves her pussy smooth like a little girl's? Got a little mole on the right inside lip. Did you know that? Hm? You ever get some of that? I'ma tell you what—that bitch is a *tasty* piece a ass, n'mean?"

Miller bounces from foot to foot. He chews on his lip, killing Frank with his eyes. She pushes him, licking her lips, singsonging, "Yeah, I ate her up like she was a piece a chocolate cake. Then I went and saw yo mama. She went down on me like she was a vulcha. That bitch be old, but she can suck a marble though a straw. She ever do you like—"

"Shut the fuck up!"

Miller feigns a lunge, and Frank steps back, laughing. "Wait a minute, little man. I ain't *even* finished. Lemme tell you what I done

54

to yo mama with *my* fo-fo. I put the barrel in her ho-ho." She makes a twisting motion with her wrist, chuckling. "Turned it nice and slo-slo. Had the bitch beggin' for mo-mo, screamin' on the flo-flo. Yeah! Tadow!"

Frank laughs and Miller breaks for her with a wild roundhouse. Frank's ready and sidesteps while slamming him into the wall. With her forearm against his Adam's apple she jams her Beretta between his teeth. In a hot rush she envisions pulling the trigger and leaving nothing of his face but neck bone and a wall stain.

"I could kill you right now," she hisses in his ear. "Call it self-defense and not lose a second's sleep over you. In fact, I'd sleep *better*. I been cleaning up after shit-scum like you my entire life. Why shouldn't I blow one more motherfuckin' puke outta this world? Huh?"

She shoves the barrel farther down his throat and he gags.

"You throw up on me you punk-ass son-of-a-bitch and I swear I'll pull this fucking trigger. How do you like being on *this* end of the gun, baby killer? Still feel like a big man? You think Clyde Payson liked it? Huh? Huh? Answer me, motherfucker!"

She bounces his head into the wall and he sputters blood with a garbled response.

"That's right, you fucking coward, he probably didn't like staring into your four-four any more than you like sucking on this Beretta. Or do you like it? I can't tell. I think you like it, you cock-sucking bitch."

The stench of Miller's piss reaches her nose and Frank looks pointedly at the mess on the floor.

"At least Payson didn't piss his pants like a fuckin' baby. Puke like you, your mother should've eaten you at birth."

Extracting the Beretta, she drops her arm and slams his head once more. Crying and choking, Miller crumples into his pool of piss. Frank stares in profound disgust, directed more at herself than at Miller. Bobby comes up to re-cuff him and Frank steps aside. The Beretta dangles from her hand.

55

"Come on. Let's go." Bobby coaxes Miller to his feet. Even after he's led the boy from the room Frank still doesn't move.

Behind her, Darcy asks, "You all right?"

No, she thinks. Definitely not all right. She turns to face her cop. "That was stupid," she says. "There was no excuse."

"Whatever. The fucking punk had it coming."

"No. Not whatever. Never whatever. You excuse it once, you'll excuse it again. Next thing you know, you're the same fucking scum they are. Only with a badge. No excuses, Darcy. We're supposed to protect people from shit-birds like Miller, not become them."

"Suit yourself." He shrugs.

"Go help your partner," she tells him.

The room is empty and Frank takes the edge of the bed. She's got the post-adrenaline shakes, and she's scared. She could have killed Miller. She *wanted* to. The tiniest flinch on her part would have spattered that bastard into whatever sorry afterlife he has coming. Frank tastes his blood on her lips and leaps up.

"Jesus!"

She paces a short, taut circle, wondering what is wrong with her. When the magpie women enter the room to upbraid her, Frank flees past them. Outside, she is comforted by the relative safety of patrol cars and uniforms. Leaving Darcy and Bobby to process the arrest she heads for the Alibi. She's still shaky by the time she gets there. Taking a stool, she orders, "Double Chivas, Mac. Make it two."

"Ice?"

She shakes her head. "Neat."

"You got it."

She swallows the first drink in one shot.

The evening crowd hasn't come in yet and Nancy perches on the stool next to her. "Hey," Frank says, relieved at the distraction. "How you doing?"

"Good. How about you?"

"Peachy-keen," Frank lies. She finishes the second glass and lifts it for a refill.

Nancy asks, "Are we drinking dinner?"

"Just the appetizer. I'll get something in a little bit."

But in a little bit Johnnie comes in. She orders Chivas for them both and when Mac pours his drink, Johnnie gripes, "Damn it, how come bartenders are all always called Mac?"

"Because we're all Scotch-Irish bastards. MacPeters, MacDougal, MacPhilips. You dumb WASP bastards can't keep us straight so you call all of us Mac."

"To dumb WASP bastards," Johnnie toasts.

Mac pours a shot to join in the toast. "To Scotch-Irish bastards." They look at Frank who hasn't raised her glass.

"Got something against the Scotch-Irish?" Mac grins.

"Nope. Just bastards in general." She changes the subject. "Mac, if you're such a good Scotch-Irish lad tell me what Chivas means."

"Oh." Mac clutches his chin. "I heard once."

"Detective Briggs, any guesses?"

"Good times ahead," Johnnie answers.

Frank shakes her head. "Guess again." It's a game she used to play with Noah—three guesses, each sillier than the next, but Johnnie doesn't know the rules.

"I don't know."

Frank peers at the amber liquor in her glass. "It's Gaelic. Means the narrow place."

"So?"

"So nothing." She sighs. "Never mind."

Chapter 13

Every witness pulls Miller out of the six-pack of photos. In the lineup, each one points and says, "That's him." He is bound over and pleads not guilty. Frank apologizes to Bobby as she did to Darcy. Nothing is said of it again, for which Frank is grateful. The calculated violence of her attack on Miller scared her and she just wants to forget it, chalk it up to circumstance and move on.

The City of Angels obliges her. After a four-year dip, violent crime stats throughout L.A. are climbing to new highs. It's only May, yet Figueroa already has 58 homicides on the books. It's a tough enough load for a full squad, and Frank's shy a man. Her best man.

Notwithstanding a brutal seventy-hour week, by the end of it Frank sits alone in her office. She has finished combing through the Pryce murder books. She has analyzed crime scene photos, autopsy reports, lab reports completed prior to losing the physical evidence, responding officer and primary detective reports, notes from Noah and canvassing officers, statements from friends, family, neighbors and the woman who found the bodies. Dozens of rap sheets have been read—from Peeping Toms to sadists to child offenders. Everything has been reviewed but the box of interview tapes. They sit in their shoebox, carefully dated and labeled in Noah's hand. She still can't bring herself to listen to them, rationalizing that Noah would have documented anything worth hearing. It's a weak argument but the best she can muster.

Frank's made her own extensive notes. Heedless of her exhaustion, she uses these to flesh out the chart she started at the beginning of her investigation. She fills in the facts to create a physical profile of the perp. Going on the assumption that the man who raped Ladeenia is the same person who killed her makes the perp a male. And he's a fit male, able to carry the bodies to the dumpsite with ease, and to snap Trevor's neck like a twig.

Perpetrators tend to feel more comfortable offending within their own race, so she labels the perp black. For the time being this is supported by the fact that a white or Asian male in a mixed black and Hispanic neighborhood would have been conspicuous and likely noted.

Race and gender are easy, but before she can construct a psychological description of her perp, she has to classify the type of crime it was. Organized or disorganized. It has elements of both, but on the whole it fits the description of an organized offense.

Frank starts with what little she can tell from the abduction. Ladeenia's visit to Cassie's was spontaneous. If the perp had known about it he wouldn't have had much time to plan around it, meaning the abduction itself was relatively spontaneous. Spontaneity is characteristic of disorganized offenders, but the abduction itself seems very well organized, not obviously sloppy or chaotic. The perp was able to plan an abduction and carry it off without calling attention to himself. This tells her the offender's intelligence is at least average, if not higher.

Snatching two kids from the street in broad daylight is a ballsy move. There are a number of ways he could have done it. One would be to lure them into a vehicle and go off with them. Mrs. Pryce said there's no way Ladeenia would get into a car with a strange man. Absolutely no way. Frank knew kids were readily swayed, but for a couple reasons she agreed that the perp probably hadn't used a vehicle.

One, it's not likely that a guy this organized would impulsively snatch not one but two kids in the middle of the afternoon. The risks were huge. He'd have to physically secure them, transport them to a private location, carry the bodies back to the car when he was done, then dump them. All this without anyone's noticing. Risky as hell. It didn't fit with his organizational skills.

Second, if he was just cruising for a likely vic, he wouldn't be cruising in his own neighborhood. The level of planning indicates he'd be smart enough to troll someplace where he wouldn't be recognized. Yet the kids were taken and dumped within a one-mile radius. This would indicate the perp had a reason to be in the area. Because both sites were residential, it seemed likely he lived within the vicinity of either site. Maybe he lived outside the area and had been trolling, but then why bring them back here for the dump? It didn't make sense to return here.

"Unless it's that remorse thing," she murmurs to her knuckles.

Frank drums her pencil on the table. This is the part she can't reconcile. The way he arranged the bodies indicates some degree of concern for the children, maybe even regret, yet is completely inconsistent with the assault and abduction. He raped Ladeenia vaginally and anally but did nothing to depersonalize her. Her face wasn't touched. She didn't appear to have been covered. Typical of assaults by strangers. The vic is simply a convenient object. The perp evinced no compassion during either assault. He didn't notice or care that her thumb was burned. She might have gotten the bruise line on the back of her leg while he raped her vaginally, again showing no compassion, no concern.

None of the evidence suggests Trevor's eyes or head were covered. He probably saw the entire assault on Ladeenia. It would be too risky to leave him out of sight. Seeing his sister attacked would have been a huge trauma for the boy, and completely thoughtless, even sadistic, on the part of the offender. The assaults on Ladeenia are vicious, but not necessarily sadistic. A sadistic rapist *has* to hurt other people to get off. Without pain, there is no excitement for the sadist. He often enacts convoluted fantasies, and tortures his victims before and/or during the assault. Pain is critical to his arousal. Ladeenia's perp obviously hurt her, but he didn't inflict pain incidental to his primary objective of rape. There is no evidence of prolonged or exaggerated cruelty.

Experts recognize four general categories of rapist, the sadistic offender being one type. Frank dismisses this category as well as the power-reassurance rapist. Perps in this category are the "gentleman rapists" who show concern for their victims during the attack. A third typology, the power-assertive rapist, gets off by being in control. These are self-obsessed offenders who feel entitled to pleasure at the cost of another's pain, deserving to fuck whomever, whenever. Because they are into control they often bind their victims. They tend to pick random rather than known targets and are often violent. Ladeenia's perp didn't appear overly aggressive, but how tough would you have to be to intimidate a nine-year-old?

The fourth category, anger-retaliatory, doesn't fit with the evidence. Anger is the motivation for these rapists, and their victims are usually badly beaten. Other than the rape, there was no excessive trauma or humiliation to Ladeenia. The assault was bloodless literally and figuratively. Frank would expect to see a lot more damage if her perp was a raging, blitz-style personality.

She considers whether he is a genuine pedophile or merely opportunistic. From her experience, child molesters who prey on prepubescent kids usually aren't gender-specific. Molesters who prey on older kids are. Her perp didn't seem to have any sexual interest in Trevor, only Ladeenia. She thinks if he were a genuine pedophile, he'd have gotten off with both kids.

"Double your pleasure, double your fun," she thinks aloud.

Consulting a number of battered texts, she decides her perp falls into various categories, which is typical of most offenders. He exhibits traits of both an organized and disorganized offender, favoring the organizational side. His style appears to be primarily power-assertive though he has attacked outside his own age range and dumped the kids in a style grossly inconsistent with that category of offender.

The lack of witnesses, the apparent speed and skill of the abduction, as well as lack of planning, all suggest Ladeenia and Trevor just happened to have chanced upon a tragic confluence of time and space.

"Seconds and inches," she mumbles. Frank shuts the binder and tips her chair back. She rocks, eyes closed. Power-assertive rapists tend to act on a cycle, allowing time for the fantasy and planning of their next rape. This perp's action was spontaneous. He saw an opportunity and literally grabbed it. The spontaneity in an otherwise highly organized crime suggests a stressor. Something may have upset him prior to the abduction, and the assault was his way of releasing that stress.

Thumping her chair down, Frank draws up a list of typical stressors. When she starts canvassing she'll inquire about neighbors' fighting, getting arrested or losing jobs, whether anyone had a recent death or divorce in the family.

The positioning of the bodies distracts Frank like a chronic, low-level pain. Their careful, almost tender placement completely contradicts the violence of the assaults. Frank considers maybe the perp was drunk when he took the kids, and the situation escalated. Next thing he knows he's got two dead kids on his hands. He didn't mean for that to happen. Just wanted a little fun. After he sobers up he is filled with remorse. He wraps the kids in the blanket. Carries them to the site. He puts them down, maybe resting for a minute, and in that minute realizes what he's done. He's emotionally exhausted and physically spent. Regret seeps into him. It's dark, so he can't see the trash on the ground, but he opens the blanket and picks the kids up, placing them next to each other. It was cold that night so he covered them with the blanket.

"Oh-h-h," she draws out. "Tenderly. Like a woman."

She plays with the idea that maybe a woman was involved. A woman who assisted in getting the kids and dumping them, then felt bad and at least left their little bodies neatly arranged. The perp would have wanted them well hidden but the woman would have wanted them found quickly. She could commiserate with the parents, wanting them to find their children quickly and in decent condition. By concealing them in the lot, they buy time, but not too much.

And Ladeenia appeared to have been raped in a kitchen, or someplace where food was served. During the autopsy the ME had collected dozens of bread crumbs and salt and sugar grains from Ladeenia's skin and from under her nails. A stain on her wrist skin turned out to be coffee mixed with sugar and creamer. Noah had noted that both parents drank their coffee black.

Frank imagines the couple taking the kids into or through the kitchen, maybe to get the duct tape, and the woman getting nervous or balking. The perp's excited. He wants to maintain control of the situation so he doesn't even give the woman a chance to protest. He rapes Ladeenia right there and then. Maybe she reaches out to hang onto something and hits the stove. Burns her thumb.

Two perps explain the crime's inconsistencies. It makes it easier to see how the kids could disappear off the sidewalk at three in the afternoon. She's pretty sure the perp is black. He likes a certain degree of regularity, control in his life. She speculates that a guy like that would want to date within his race and stick to what he knows.

"So a black couple."

The theory elicits the welcome tingle of a good lead, and Frank follows it.

"Maybe they're involved with the community."

Church-goers. The type you'd never suspect, otherwise they'd have been the first for people to point fingers at. She still thinks they're local. They have a house or apartment close to where the kids were taken. Or maybe a restaurant. That would explain the food particles, but she can't think of any food joints along the abduction route. Somehow, the couple is in the vicinity when the kids are. Their presence wouldn't be suspicious. They belonged there. No one would notice them. The woman may even have known the kids. If the man did, he didn't seem to care. And he's clearly in charge.

"A manly man."

Frank nods. It jibes with the power-assertive classification. A guy like that would have a very feminine woman. He'd tell her what to do, how to do it and when. She might have wanted children but he wouldn't allow it. He wouldn't want to share her. His woman would be petite, attractive and subservient. Well-groomed and well-dressed. Her femininity would make him look even more masculine. He'd have a macho ride, something souped up and tricked out, a late-model muscle car. Image is a big deal to this guy.

"But such a big deal," she argues with herself, "that he probably wouldn't bother attacking children."

It would make him look small. He would probably prey on well-developed older girls or young women. Unless he's got that stressor going on. Has a fight with the little woman. Sees the kids and is in a good position to take them. Wants to do something to feel good about himself, reassert his power and authority, his manliness. Ladeenia's little, but what a coup snatching *two* kids would be. That'd show everyone what a stud he was.

Frank tips her chair again, pleased as a kid with a new toy. A good profiler needs to be flexible. Frank learned that during her sabbatical at Quantico. Getting fixed on a single track usually derails a profiling effort. Rigidity makes it impossible to tweak and rearrange data. Frank's been profiling a single perp. Now she has to switch tracks and look for a couple. She drums the chair's arm with the pencil.

"*No problema*," she tells the ceiling. The case is six years old and Frank has nothing but time. Amused at her folly, she smiles. Of course there is no one to see it.

Chapter 14

Gail has to run downtown and she calls Frank to meet her for lunch.

Frank lies, "I'm kind of tied up, but thanks for asking."

"Okay. I'll see you tonight then. Want me to get dinner?"

"Actually, I'm going to have dinner with Trace and the kids."

"Oh."

Gail's disappointment is obvious in that one, small word. For the merest second, Frank feels like a real shit. Then she feels nothing.

"Well, I guess I'll see you when you get here."

"Yeah. Don't wait up. I'll slip in next to you."

Frank is glad to hang up. Gail's voice used to be enough to soothe the cold, dark places inside of Frank, but lately not even Gail's touch can penetrate those lonely hollows. She saw a stone quarry once, in upstate New York. It was winter. She was on a school field trip. The quarry was fenced off and abandoned. Steep, gray pits had been left to fill with snow. Dark pines brooded above the holes. The bloodless sky matched the cold rock. Her classmates went quiet, hushed by the stillness of wind on stone. Frank wonders if a surgeon were to cut her open, would he find just rock and snow?

Irritated, Frank shakes away the image. She has things to do before dinner. When she arrives at Noah's, Tracey is overjoyed.

Frank says, "You've lost weight, mama."

"Yeah. One of the advantages of grief," Tracey replies, not without rancor. Frank plays Munch's Oddysee with the younger kids while Tracey puts dinner out. When she goes upstairs to get Leslie, she returns without her.

"Not eating?" Frank asks. Tracey shakes her head with a helplessness that breaks Frank's heart. She wrestles with her cowardice before asking, "Can I go talk to her?"

"What are you gonna say?"

Markie sits at the table playing with army men and Jamie meticulously lays out napkins.

"That I know how it feels."

Memory surfaces in Tracey's eyes. She nods and Frank slips up the stairs.

"Yeah?" Leslie says to the knock on her door.

"Hey. Not hungry?"

Leslie wags her head and Frank balances next to her on the edge of the bed. Noah's oldest daughter is all giraffe legs and stick arms, skinny like her dad. She'll bust hearts someday and Frank hates that Noah won't be there to fret over her first date or give his daughter away when she marries. She hates this whole fucked-up situation and cuts straight to the point.

"You miss your dad pretty bad?" Leslie shrugs. She doesn't look up from the book in her lap, so Frank admits, "I do. He was my best friend."

The admission gets her nowhere. But for Noah's sake Frank tries another tack. She pulls in a deep, silent breath, sounding before she dives into the benthic mess of emotion.

"I know how you feel, Les. When I was about your age, maybe a little younger, more like Jamie's age, my dad died, too. It was real quick. One minute he was there and the next he was gone. I felt like the whole world had ended. I thought I was gonna die too. I wanted to."

Leslie's hair hangs over her face. Frank tucks a curtain of it behind a rather large ear. Les is a beauty but she got her daddy's ears. This vestige of Noah is sharp and wickedly painful, but Frank pushes through her discomfort. She will see this through, for Leslie and for Noah.

"You ever feel like that?"

The head bobs.

"Yeah. You will for a while. It feels bad for a long time. But then one day, and you don't know which day it'll be, you'll wake up and you'll forget to feel bad. You'll remember later in the day, and you'll feel bad, but then it'll go away again. The hurt gets softer and softer."

Leslie offers no indication she's heard.

Frank asks, "Remember when you broke your ankle, how bad it hurt?"

"Yeah."

"Does it hurt today?"

"No."

"But it hurt for a while after you broke it, didn't it?"

"Yeah."

"That's what this is like. I know it sucks big-time, but I promise it'll get better someday."

A droplet falls onto the open book and Leslie whispers, "I want someday to be today."

Taking Leslie's hand, Frank whispers back, "I know. But it can't be. It's impossible. Like having your ankle fixed right away. It took time. This will too. But it *will* get better. I promise."

Frank wipes Leslie's cheeks with her thumbs and Leslie blurts, "I want him back."

"I know, Les. Me too. We all do. But we can't have him back. Now it's just you and Markie and Jamie and your mom. And you gotta love each other even more to fill that empty space your dad left."

"Nothing can fill that." She gulps.

Frank cradles the little chin between both her hands. She speaks the words without thinking them, and will wonder later where they came from. "Love will. You gotta trust me on this. I know it doesn't seem like it right now, but if you love each other enough, that hole's going to fill up someday. It may not fill completely up. No one can ever replace your dad, but I promise it won't hurt quite this bad." Looking into the pools of hurt that are Leslie's young eyes, Frank knows she can't stay much longer. "Do you trust me?"

Leslie nods.

"Okay. Come on downstairs. Your family misses you. Your mom needs her oldest girl and Markie and Jamie need their big sister."

Leslie lets Frank lead her downstairs. While Tracey dishes spaghetti at the table Frank disappears into the kitchen. She opens another bottle of wine, chugging an entire glass before returning to the dining room. Tracey smiles her thanks as Frank realizes the only empty chair is Noah's. She fills Tracey's glass, then her own.

"Do you want me to sit there?"

Tracey waves her toward it. Mark and Leslie stare and Jamie says, "It's okay."

"Okay with you, Les?"

"No one else is there." She pouts.

"Right," Frank agrees.

The talk during dinner is quiet but easy. Frank marvels how Trace and the kids neither avoid Noah nor dwell on him. Later, Frank does the dishes while Tracey tucks the kids in bed. The two bottles of wine that Frank brought are empty. She opens a third soldier that Tracey produced, a cheap but serviceable Cab. Finished in the kitchen, she waits for Tracey at the table. She swirls the wine in her glass, watching it run down the sides. Frank is thinking this is more entertaining than a lava lamp when Tracey lays a hand on her shoulder and asks, "Where's mine?"

Frank smiles and retrieves a glass, appreciating that Tracey can match her drink for drink. "Everyone settled in?"

Tracey nods. "What did you say to Les?"

"Not much. Just told her about my dad."

"What happen—"

Frank raises a hand, warning, "Don't even go there. I just told her it was going to be bad for a while, then it'll get better." Steering the conversation, Frank notes, "I was watching you at dinner. You're great with the kids. You're a great mom. Noah loved that about you."

Tracey's head falls, and her voice wobbles as she insists, "I don't know how great I am. I feel like I use the kids to keep from thinking about him. But nighttime's the worst. God! When dinner's done, baths are done, they're asleep. That's the worst. When it's just me. And when I wake up and I've forgotten, and then it all comes crashing back in, just the horrible, awful loneliness of it over and over again, brand new each time. That's the worst and I wonder how I can possibly get out of bed. But then the kids wake up and they're hungry, so I get up, and I get dressed and dress them, and we eat and get out the door and life goes on. One goddamn meal and one goddamn minute at a time."

Tracey swipes her tears with her palm. She gets up and clatters around the kitchen for a few minutes. She returns with a bowl of cherries.

"Noah hated cherries," she says with a pale grin.

"In a pie, he'd have said, and wiggled his eyebrows like Groucho."

"Yeah, yeah." Tracey waves. "He was all talk."

The joking disappears and Tracey leans closer to Frank.

"Wasn't he? Did he ever cheat on me? I know cops can get laid like that—" She snaps her fingers. "Did he ever—"

"Absolutely not." Frank is shaking her head. "He wouldn't have. He *couldn't* have, Trace. He loved you. Loved the kids too much. The guilt would've killed him." Tracey sits back, and Frank throws in, "Besides. You were a good wife. He didn't have any reason to go elsewhere."

"I hope so. He was a good husband."

They are quiet, fiddling with the cherries.

At length Tracey says, "Did I ever tell you I can tie a cherry stem with my tongue?"

"Couple times. I ever show you a lesbian with a hard-on?"

Tracey bulges her cheek out with her tongue and Frank grins.

"I was so jealous of you when we were first married. He had *such* a crush on you."

"Yeah."

Noah had always been respectful with his ardor and Frank had gracefully ignored it. His passion eventually died for lack of fuel and what took its place was their friendship. Sitting here next to his wife, it occurs to Frank that Noah *did* have an affair. With her. Not a conventional one, surely, but an affair that endured all these years nonetheless. Tracey is watching her, and Frank knows she's seen the naked thought when she asks, "Is there something I should know about that?"

"No. Never anything like that. You know that."

Frank envies Tracey and Leslie their tears. She feels them churning inside her and wants to blurt how much Noah loved her and how much she loved him. How she took for granted that he'd always be there. Always interfering, always telling Frank what to do. Saying what she couldn't. And still can't.

Frank clamps her teeth together, but a quaver still escapes when she reminds Tracey, "It's late. We've gotta work tomorrow." She drains her glass and stands.

Tracey stands with her, taking Frank into a hug. "You love him as much as I do."

The tears make a final stand against their stony prison walls, but Frank is prepared, quelling the surge before it can rally. "Maybe." She shrugs. "Different, but maybe."

She kisses Tracey good-bye. It will be a long time before she comes back.

Chapter 15

The dumpsite hasn't changed. A useless, handwritten sign warns, NO GARBAGE. Crude paths transect the lot. Frank looks at a crime scene photo from the same angle it was taken. There's no path in the picture.

Frank steps into the cored ruin, checking it against a couple of pictures. It's gone now, but there was a mattress about ten feet from where the bodies were found. Frank thinks the perp dumped the kids on the ground, but that the woman took the time to arrange them properly. She'd have felt remorse, but he would have been trying to hustle her out. She wasn't familiar enough with the site to have him at least put the kids on the mattress. A guy like that wouldn't be secure enough to leave his wife alone for very long. They probably did everything together, so Frank assumes he's equally unfamiliar with what's behind the improvised walls. They probably know the dumpsite in passing but never stepped foot in it until they left the kids there. This reinforces Frank's suspicion that her perps live in the neighborhood and lead relatively respectable lives. They aren't junkies or loonies crawling around in abandoned buildings.

Frank wanders the lot in a grid. She picks her way around broken bottles and chunks of concrete. Dried weeds brush against her legs. Their seeds hitchhike on her socks and trousers. She wonders if there are ticks. Gail would know. She'd probably laugh at Frank's squeamishness, and for an instant Frank regrets the distance she's put between them.

Having walked the entire lot, she surveys it from different angles. The perp would have been vulnerable from the north where the lot faces the street, and from the house on the west overlooking the site. High fences on the east and south block the view. Frank knows that the house directly across the street was vacant when the Pryce kids were dumped. Not a bad gamble to dump two bodies here. Especially in a part of the city where no one minds anyone else's business, and if they do, they don't tell.

But why not farther away? Frank wonders. The perps were obviously mobile enough to get the kids here, so why not keep going and hide them really well? Organized offenders usually make some attempt to hide the bodies. The Pryce attempt was half-assed, leading again to the idea of two perps. Frank thinks the woman might have pleaded to leave the children close to home, in a place where they'd be found quickly. The thought of the children rotting and being eaten by animals might have been so disturbing that for once she argued with her man. He might have been distracted enough to cave. He would have been anxious to get rid of the bodies. If the abduction was as spontaneous as it seemed, he wouldn't have planned out a disposal site. The lot probably put a comfortable enough distance from where they lived, or from wherever they abducted the kids, while concealing the bodies in the rubble bought them time to clean up.

She is mindful as she walks that one of Ladeenia's shoes was found next to a sprung sofa. It appeared that the shoe had snagged off her foot in passing. Either the killer hadn't noticed or didn't care. Probably the latter as he was no doubt in a hurry and what evidence would there be in a shoe? But it tells Frank her perp is tall enough to carry Ladeenia so that her foot dangled at the height of the couch. It's also in the back of her mind that Ladeenia's panties were never found. Frank has thought about this.

Power-assertive rapists, as she has tentatively classified her perp, don't usually take trophies, but it's possible this is one of the ways her perp doesn't completely fit the profile. Frank's hope is that whoever killed Ladeenia kept her underwear. It's a long shot, she knows, and she mumbles, "If wishes were horses . . ."

Frank is so deep in thought that she reminds herself to ask Noah if Mrs. Pryce might know what was in Trevor's pockets. Then memory guts her like a switchblade. Her immediate reaction to the pain is fury. It mutates into helplessness. Frank swallows it down, all the hot little knives. She clenches her teeth and stares at a tag on the south fence. She will absolutely not lose it and certainly not here.

Noah was rarely in the office after the case went down. When she'd catch up to him, he'd explain this was where he'd been, probing inch by inch through garbage, dog shit and weeds, climbing up on rooftops to survey the scene from that vantage, sitting for endless hours amid the cold debris. This is where he'd been. And for Frank, this is where he still is. She's awed by how much she misses him.

Frank blinks hard, forging her composure on the anvil of deliberation. The transformation is made manifest—her jaw unclenches, shoulders drop and fingers relax. The effort is exhausting, but Frank disregards this too. Stoic the Magnificent is back and at the top of her game. She continues through her grids as if nothing has happened.

For the next few weeks Frank runs on alcohol, caffeine and a smoldering rage. Pacing the cage of her office, she is Blake's "tiger, tiger burning bright." Her detectives give her a wide berth. She can feel their edginess around her. Though they would never admit it, they are probably afraid of her, afraid of being in her line of fire if and when she should blow. And they're likely even more nervous that whatever Frank has might be contagious, so they keep their distance.

Frank helps. She does what she has to do in the office as quickly as possible then heads for Raymond Street. Unless she has a meeting or gets called to a homicide, she is gone all day. She has become a regular fixture in the neighborhood. The crazy-ass white bitch walking up and down the street late afternoons is such a familiar sight that the dopers smoking on stoops don't even bother hiding their chronic. The really perking ones might call out to her, but an ugly void in Frank's eye keeps them where they are.

She mad-dogs each house. One of them must have borne witness to Ladeenia and Trevor's abduction. She curses that she can't get wood to speak. Prowling the sidewalk day after day, she waits for the houses to yield their secrets. She can't envision what the sign, the clue, will look like, yet she walks and waits for the burning bush that will crack the case. When it doesn't appear, she's not disappointed. Burning bushes work on their own schedule.

Frank has drawn multi-colored lines on a map. The festive lines connect the Pryces' house to Cassie Bertram's duplex in myriad configurations. The most direct route is marked with a fat red line. Frank believes this is the route Ladeenia would have chosen. Her reasoning is simple; it was late in the day and Ladeenia would have wanted to spend her time with Cassie, not wandering along indirect routes. Plus, the cold weather and threatening rain would have added to Ladeenia's haste. So Frank walks the red line. She checks alleys and yards. She knocks on every door, questioning the occupants along the route.

Most of the people she talks to don't want to talk to her. They have already talked to the police. To Noah, to the uniforms that canvassed with him, to Noah again. Frank reminds them that South Central residents accuse cops of not caring, not trying hard enough. Here it is six years later, she stresses, and we're still looking for whoever did this to these kids. We haven't forgotten. She flaps Ladeenia and Trevor's smiling school photos. They talk. But it's been a long time. They add nothing that's not anecdotal from the media. Some don't remember and others didn't live here then. But Frank doesn't get discouraged. She expects as much. The case is old. People forget. But she has to satisfy herself that she has talked to every possible witness, every potential suspect.

A second, longer line on Frank's map stretches from the red line to the dumpsite. She will start questioning people along the most direct route, working backward from the site to the home where the Pryces lived at the time of the abduction. Then she will canvass secondary routes, and tertiary. More if necessary. She is determined to cover a wide radius between the two lines.

She studies the dozens of photos Noah took of the crime scene and neighborhood. She carries pictures of onlookers from the crowd with her. Noah's already identified most of them. Frank makes everyone she questions study the faces in the photos. One man identifies his brother. He's moved to Las Vegas. The man Frank talks to can't remember what *he* was doing the night the Pryces were murdered, let alone his brother.

Frank tracks the brother down. Jorge Medina. He buses tables at the Riviera Casino. He has a history of misdemeanors and fails to return Frank's phone calls. On a starry Saturday morning she drives to Las Vegas to catch Medina during his noon shift. Medina's an unimpressive character who remembers nothing. He racks his brain but can't tell Frank what he was doing that night six years ago. He doesn't even remember why he was visiting his brother. When he lived in Orange County it wasn't unusual for their families to get together and have dinner, play cards. Frank watches his apprehension grow in proportion to the failure of his memory.

Finally she flips him her business card, tells him to call if he thinks of anything. She leaves with the conviction he's clueless. Civilians are naturally nervous around cops, but only guilty people try to hide their worry. In addition, barring a traumatic event in their lives, the only people who can tell you what they were doing on a given night six years past are people who have created an alibi and memorized it. Innocent people don't need alibis.

Frank leaves Las Vegas no closer to a suspect than when she arrived. Still she's pleased with the miles of desert highway between her and L.A. Plenty of hours to think about the Pryce kids. Hot air blows through the car and she cools off with a six-pack of Coronas triple-bagged around a bag of ice. Frank slaps her hand against the door, keeping time with ZZ Top and Stevie Ray Vaughn. Well insulated, she cruises into the burning sunset.

Chapter 16

Despite a traffic jam in Barstow, Gail is still awake when Frank gets in from Vegas. She puts down the book she is reading and smiles.

"Any luck?"

"Nope. Guy didn't know a thing."

"Sorry."

Heading for the bathroom, Frank shrugs. "No big. I'm gonna get the dust off of me."

She spends as much time as she can in the shower, hoping Gail will be asleep by the time she's done. But she isn't and Frank gets into bed beside her. Gail closes her book and turns the light off. She snuggles into Frank, and Frank accommodates the doc's head on her shoulder. Gail caresses Frank in a way that used to drive her nutty. Now Gail's touch is almost repulsive. She's relieved when Gail quits.

"Talk to me," Gail whispers to Frank.

Except for a mad desire to be back on the highway, Frank feels nothing.

"I can't," she confesses.

"Why not?"

"I just can't. There aren't any words inside me."

"Just empty?" Gail sympathizes.

Frank thinks again about the frozen quarry. "Yeah. All empty."

This seems to satisfy Gail but then she asks, "Is it Noah? Is it still missing him so much?"

The answer that leaps to mind is *worse*, and Frank is furious. Furious at Gail for bringing up what she's worked so hard to ignore, furious at this invasion of privacy, furious that Gail cares, furious that she can't go to sleep, furious that she has to constantly defend herself. Inside, she is a raging ball of self-contained fiery hell. Outside she is a sheet of glass—cold, rigid and just as fragile.

"I can't talk about this," she manages.

"Why? What would happen if you did?"

"You're asking the impossible, Gail. Do you want to see me crack into a million pieces? Is that what you want? To see me all busted up like Humpty Dumpty? You'd be stuck with a thousand broken pieces and you'd have to sweep me up with a broom and put all my pieces into a paper bag where they'd scream for all eternity, and you'd have to hear that and I'd have to hear that and we'd go crazy with all the endless screaming. Is that what you want?"

Gail soothes, "Do you really believe that?"

"Yeah. I do. Don't ask me to go there."

Frank feels Gail nod. Still she asks, "Would the same thing happen if you talked to Clay?"

"Don't you remember? Once Humpty Dumpty breaks, it's all over. No one could put him back together again. Not all the King's horses, not all the King's men. He shattered beyond all hope. If he'd just stayed on the wall, he'd have been all right. So I'm hanging on to the wall."

"What if the wall's crumbling?"

"The wall's not crumbling," Frank insists. "Humpty Dumpty had a great fall. He jumped or slipped. Maybe he was pushed, but the wall didn't break."

"Frank, Humpty Dumpty's a fairy tale, and you're not an egg. If you break, you'll heal. If you don't break, you won't heal. Don't you know that by now? Isn't that what happened with Maggie. You *didn't* break and look what happened. You ended up in Clay's office. He broke you properly, like a bone that was badly set, and helped you mend. You've got to break in order to get everything out or you'll explode trying to keep all it in. Do you want to go through all that again?"

Frank argues, "Fairy tales are metaphors for real life. If Humpty had just minded his own business and paid attention to staying on that wall he'd have been okay. But he slipped. He started snooping around in places where he had no business. He was an egg trying to be something he wasn't. I'm a cop, trying to pretend I'm not. I'm trying to pretend I can live like other people. That I can deal with life by talking and feeling, and I can't. For me to do what I've got to do I can't feel it and I can't talk about it. I've got to bag up my shit and dump it like the trash it is. Then forget about it. I'm hanging on to the wall, Gail. I'm bagging up the trash. I'm not going to fall off into that touchy-feely never-never land. I tried that. It doesn't work for me."

"Oh, I see. Alcoholism and workaholism are so much healthier. Is that it?"

"How many times do we have to have this conversation?" Frank sighs into the dark.

"You tell me."

"You're the one that keeps bringing it up."

Gail separates her body from Frank's. She lies motionless on her side of the bed. Frank silently begs Gail to fall asleep. She believes her wish has been granted until Gail demands, "Are you satisfied with our relationship?"

Lacing her fingers under her head, Frank breathes, "Fuck."

She should have known better. Gail's a pit bull in an argument.

"Are you?"

"Not right now, no."

"Generally?"

"Generally it's fine."

"Tell me what you like about it."

"Gail, why are you doing this?"

"Because I need to know. What do you like about our relationship? From what I can see, it doesn't look like much. Half the time you beg off seeing me, and when you do deign to grace me with your presence you're remote, aloof and unapproachable."

Frank notes the triple redundancy of Gail's description, thereby making her guilty of only one fault.

"And in case you haven't noticed, we haven't made love since Noah died. I don't think you even like breathing the same air as me! But you're perfectly happy."

Guilty as charged, Frank thinks. Gail is absolutely right. Frank doesn't want to be with her. It's more effort than she can manage right now. It's not fair to drag Gail down to her level, but neither is it sporting of Gail to demand Frank meet her bar. Searching the air above the bed, Frank knows she must choose. Gail or the wall. Falling or staying. She makes her decision, but her words are halting.

"You deserve better, Gail. Someone who can go through things with you. I can't. I just can't. I'm not built that way. I'm sorry." She rolls her back to Gail. "Good night."

To ensure she won't fall, Frank has crucified herself to the wall.

Chapter 17

Frank's commute always gives her time to reflect, and the next morning she will go so far as to say she's a heavy drinker and sometimes she drinks too much. Who doesn't? But there is drinking, and then there's problem drinking. If drinking doesn't interfere with her daily functions, then there's no problem. If it does interfere, then it's a problem. Frank can't see how her drinking is a problem. She does the same things that teetotalers do—she gets to work on time, does a good job, pays her bills and keeps her house up. What more does Gail want?

To prove she has no problem, Frank vows to stay sober for a week. If she can get through the week without seeing purple spiders or ending up in the Betty Ford clinic, then she must be okay. If she can't, then she has a problem. She tests herself the week Foubarelle goes out of town. Being on call the whole week is good incentive to stay sober. The days are easy, the nights a little harder. Around four or five o'clock, her body nags that it's time for a drink. She distracts herself with work. She spends the hours interviewing residents along the street where the Pryce family used to live. She knocks as late as eight o'clock and then spends another couple hours writing notes. Twice she sleeps on the skinny vinyl couch in her office. The other nights she slips in next to Gail for what is little more than a nap and change of clothes.

When Fubar returns, Frank celebrates her week of sobriety at the Alibi. Tossing off a double, she orders another. Johnnie joins her and at midnight Nancy asks, "Want me to call you a cab?"

Frank thinks, *you can call me anything you like,* but says, "Good idea."

Next morning her hangover is exquisite. She wonders how she got that drunk. She didn't mean to, and scolds that she should've had dinner. She resolves to go easy tonight. Two beers, max, she tells herself.

Alcohol has always been a friend Frank can count on. When she feels low it consoles her. When she wants to celebrate it takes her higher. When she mourns, it comforts her. When she needs to chill, it calms her. If she's a little down, it brings her up. If she's amped too high, it brings her down. The booze oils her enough to fit comfortably into her own skin, no matter how tight, how large, how raw or how exhilarated she feels. It makes bad times bearable and good times better.

Because the booze has always been such a loyal and dependable friend, Frank cannot—will not—see its betrayal. And the betrayals start off small enough: a hangover on a workday, the fuzzily recalled evening, a tiff that in the sober light of dawn seems senseless. They're *petite mignons,* really, little sins, of fleeting concern during her shower or drive to work.

Because she hasn't noticed the smaller betrayals, she's equally blind to the larger ones—the recriminating arguments that leave her bruised but justified; remorseful cold shoulders to those deserving better; the dull head that shadows much of her workday followed near the end of watch by distractive planning of what to drink and where.

Alcohol is Frank's right-hand man, her Robinson Crusoe and Gal Friday rolled into one. It's the cavalry routing the bad guys in the final desperate hour. It's the lifeline suddenly appearing in a walloping sea. So of course she has ignored all the hints and signs that her old friend is going behind her back. Who could look at that? Who would want to see? She keeps loving her buddy, her pal, sharing the bulk of her time with it and all her confidences. And her friend pats her hand or gives her the high-five just as it always has. And because she still trusts it, unable to believe it has anything but her best interests at heart, she willingly takes its hand and follows it too far.

When she wakes from a blackout wondering how she got home, while she pulls her guts up through her teeth at the kitchen sink, or hides bloodshot eyes behind Ray Bans and shaking hands in pockets, she wonders how she's crossed the line again. She berates herself for going as far as she has and swears she won't do it again. But when the booze calls her and says one or two won't hurt, just for old time's sake, she says, "Sure," certain, *trusting* even, that her old friend won't hurt her. And because she trusts it, she follows it repeatedly, again and again, over the line.

Frank decides her vow to stick to two beers is unnecessary. By nine o'clock that night she has finished a six-pack. There are no notable aftereffects and Frank thinks no more of limits or abstaining. She is fine. Just fine.

Chapter 18

There are two people that Frank has yet to talk to—Mary and Walter Pryce. She's put off calling Ladeenia and Trevor's parents because she knows they will ask about Noah. He had stayed in touch, calling them regularly just to check in. To let them know he hadn't forgotten. He'd been fond of the Pryces and they of him. Everyone liked Noah. He was just that kind of guy.

Frank has a few questions for the Pryces, loose ends she could easily tie up on the phone, but she wants to meet them. They are the living link to the case she's become so attached to. And they are a link to Noah.

She calls to arrange a meeting. Sundays, after church, is the best time for them. And the worst for Frank—Sundays are when she and Gail try to carve some time out together.

During a late dinner on Wednesday night, Frank tries killing two birds with the same stone.

"I called the Pryces today. The parents in Noah's cold case. I need to talk to them face-to-face but the only time that works for both of them is Sunday afternoons. They live up in Santa Maria, so I was wondering if you'd like to drive up there with me. I just need about twenty minutes with them, and then we can have the rest of the day to do whatever you want. Maybe have lunch in Santa Barbara, hit some antique stores?"

They are eating Chinese food at Yujean Kang's. Gail looks up from her Ants on a Tree to reach for Frank's hand. "That'd be fun. I'd like that."

Frank holds on to the hand in hers. This is the part where she should say something tender and sincere. The words themselves come easily enough after a lifetime of cajoling witnesses and suspects, but Frank is sure that if she speaks them without feeling that Gail will see right through her. She settles for squeezing the doc's hand and assuring her, "Me, too."

Sunday breaks hot and bright. They pick up coffee and cinnamon buns at Europane and head for Highway 101. Looking east, the mountains sport spring wildflowers, and to the west the Pacific sparkles benignly under a bright blue sky. It's a textbook southern California day. Gail chatters about work and her mom and sisters. Frank makes the appropriate noises and feigns interest but her thoughts are where they always are—with the Pryce case.

Leaving Gail contentedly reading in the car, Frank introduces herself to Mary and Walter Pryce. When they inevitably ask why the case has been reassigned, much as she hates to, Frank tells them the truth. The news saddens them and although they offer to help Frank however they can, their resignation is palpable.

As promised, Frank is soon back on the highway where it occurs to her that the Pryces have closed the book on their dead children and moved on. If they've moved on, why shouldn't she? Why keep flogging this dead horse? There are file cabinets back at Figueroa full of unsolved cases, some as tragic as Ladeenia and Trevor's, some more so. Why not focus on them instead?

Because this is Noah's case, comes the dim response from a corner of her brain. She tells herself she wants to solve it for him. Not for the Pryces—to hell with them—but for Noah. He'd appreciate it. But an even darker corner of her brain whispers that if she lets Pryce go, she has to let Noah go, too.

She turns to Gail and forces a smile. "So what's for lunch?"

Frank keeps her brain hushed for the next couple of weeks by spending every available minute canvassing a tight pattern of houses between Cassie Bertram's duplex and the old Pryce house. Ninety percent of the time she is off the clock.

For weeks she gets nothing but attitude and indifference. Deciding to switch to where the crime ended rather than where it started, she starts knocking on doors immediately around the dump-site. A wino and five kids have moved into the house where the woman with the chicken lived. An elderly Salvadoran couple owns the house behind the dumpsite. Two of their children and three of their grandchildren share the three-bedroom bungalow. They lived there when the Pryce kids were discovered and tsk-tsk about the tragedy that was. So many tragedies. Of course things were different when they were younger. They remember nothing Frank doesn't already know. By the time she leaves them the sun has been down for an hour. She consults her watch. Just one more.

Frank checks her notes. Yolanda Miron lives on the west side of the dumpsite. Frank sees lights on in the house and presses her luck. A gray-haired Hispanic woman opens warily at her knock. Holding up her badge and ID, Frank inquires, "Mrs. Miron?"

The woman nods with concern but as Frank explains the reason for her visit she relaxes and invites Frank in. A stout man-child with the obvious characteristics of Down's syndrome looks up at Frank as she enters the living room. Mrs. Miron says, "Izzy, it's almost bed-time. Pick up your things."

Izzy nods, complying with quick, curious looks at Frank. Frank begins by rote and Mrs. Miron echoes what everyone else has said—it's been such a long time. She's afraid she has nothing new to add. Like a few other people, she remembers Noah and asks why he's not working the case.

Frank usually answers this inquiry by saying he's been reassigned. Maybe because it's been a long day, maybe because she's frustrated, maybe because Mrs. Miron is nice and her house smells like cookies, Frank tells her Noah was killed in a car accident. Izzy overhears this and interjects, "My Papi was killed in a car."

Mrs. Miron nods. "A month before those children were found. It was such a crazy time. What with Christmas coming and my daughter getting married. She got married the weekend they found them, the children. We were all so sad without Papi. It didn't seem right without him but it seemed wrong to stop living. My husband was a very strong man, very proud. We talked about it a long time and decided Papi would want the wedding to go." Her hands flap in her lap like little birds trying to take off. She apologizes. "That's why I remember so little. It seems silly, we were right next door, but we had so much happening with ourselves."

Frank nods encouragement, watching Izzy arrange a collection of action dolls in a large laundry basket. He's laid them side by side and is covering them with a worn hand towel. He rearranges some of the figures so that eventually they are all covered, with only their heads exposed. The little hairs all along Frank's body rise in a delicious frisson. She has a wild idea. A ridiculous long shot, but she asks anyway. "Where was Izzy that weekend?"

"Oh, he was here with me. In fact, he got sick that weekend. It was one more crazy thing." Mrs. Miron's smile for Izzy turns the comment from a complaint into a statement.

"Did Detective Jantzen ever talk to Izzy about the children?"

"Oh, no." Mrs. Miron is adamant. "He was sick that weekend. I remember he was in bed. We were worried about him because a cold with him can sometimes turn into pneumonia. He's not so active and they settle in his lungs, so what with my husband's funeral and the wedding, then Izzy getting sick—"

"Detective Jantzen never talked to him later?"

"Not that I remember. Izzy's usually in school during the day. He goes to special school."

Frank watches Izzy fussing with the blanket, making sure each doll is tucked in just so. She asks, "Would you mind if I ask him a few questions? I promise I won't upset him."

"Of course," the woman says, "but I don't know how he can help. Izzy," Mrs. Miron says to claim her son's attention. "This lady would like to talk to you."

Izzy grins at Frank, and she smiles back.

"Hi, Izzy. What are you playing with?"

"These are my dolls," he answers thickly.

Frank waits while he names each one. When he's done, she says admiringly, "They're very pretty. What are you doing with them?"

"I'm putting them to bed."

"Do you do that every night?"

He nods and tugs at the hand towel. Mrs. Miron adds, "He started doing that right after his father died. We explained how dying is like a long sleep and when Izzy saw his Papi in the coffin he insisted we give him a blanket. He wouldn't stop pestering us until my son brought a blanket in from his car and let Izzy tuck it around him. Since then he tucks all his toys in, every night. Don't you?"

Izzy's nod is happy and Frank asks if Izzy was in bed the entire weekend of the Pryce killings.

Mrs. Miron answers for him. "The wedding was on Sunday and Izzy was tugging at me all day Saturday. I felt bad, what with him just losing his Papi, but we were so busy getting ready for the wedding. And then he got sick Sunday—I had to leave before they cut the cake—and I felt so bad I'd been neglecting him but there was just so much craziness."

"So he was okay Saturday?"

"Yes, he seemed fine then. I noticed his nose was runny and I gave him some yerba tea that night but it wasn't until the next day that he got the fever."

Frank pulls two pictures from her notebook. "Izzy?" She gets his full attention before saying, "I'm going to show you a picture of a boy and a girl and I want you to tell me if you've ever seen them before. Okay?"

"Okay."

Frank hands him the pictures of Ladeenia and Trevor. Even before they have left her hands, Izzy is beaming.

"I put them to bed," he announces. Jabbing a finger toward the window, he added, "I put them to bed outside. They were outside and I put them to bed."

"You put them to bed," Frank repeats slowly.

"I put them to bed outside," Izzy repeats, nodding.

Mrs. Miron is alarmed and Frank puts a hand on her arm.

"When did you do that?"

"When they were sleeping out there. In the *casita*."

"Isador!" his mother cries. "Why didn't you tell me?"

The boy the size of a man looks like he's about to cry and Frank answers, "It's okay, Izzy. Maybe that's what you were trying to tell your mother the day of the wedding."

Izzy just looks scared and confused, but Mrs. Miron sags. She throws a troubled glance toward Frank while reassuring her son. She cradles him with one arm while the hand of the other flies to her mouth.

"*Ay Dios,*" she breathes. "*Como no.* He kept going on about the *casita* and how he put the children to bed. I thought he was talking about his dolls."

Frank asks gently, "Do you remember putting the children to bed, Izzy?"

He lifts his big head up and down.

"What do you remember?"

"They were sleeping, but they weren't put to bed right. I had to put them to bed."

"Can you show me with your dolls how they were when you found them?"

Izzy glances at his mother and she nods approval.

"They were like this," he says, taking two of the dolls and wrapping them together one atop the other in the towel.

"What did you do with them?"

"I put them like this."

He puts the dolls side by side again, covering them to their chins. "I put them to bed."

"One more question," Frank says more for his mother's benefit than for Izzy's. It's the holdback question. The one only someone who has seen the bodies can answer.

"Was there anything on their faces? Anything that maybe shouldn't have been there?"

Izzy fades for a moment then pumps his big head furiously. "They had tapes on their mouths. Gray tapes. It was on their mouths. Like this."

Izzy draws a circle around his head with his finger. He returns Frank's smile.

Chapter 19

Based on Izzy Miron's new information, Frank revises her suspect profile. After his initial revelation he didn't have much more to add. In retrospect, Mrs. Miron remembered shooing him out of the house because it was sunny and telling him not to go out of the yard. But Izzy was fascinated with the abandoned lot next door and frequently snuck over. Sometimes nice kids were there, sometimes mean kids. That Saturday morning it was dead kids. Only Izzy didn't know that. He just knew they were sleeping a long time. People that slept a long time couldn't talk, like his Papi and his dolls.

The children were wrapped in a blanket but Izzy carefully undid them and laid them side by side. They were just like big dolls. Only their blanket smelled like his sister's boyfriend. Mrs. Miron explained that meant the blanket smelled like smoke, which Noah had made reference to in his notes.

After hearing Izzy's story it made sense to Mrs. Miron why her son had been pestering her for a blanket for his new dolls. She wouldn't give him a blanket to take outside, it was too muddy, and she'd tried to distract him with a Barney video and his coloring books. Eventually he'd settled down. The next day he'd gotten sick and been in bed for three days. By the time he got back to the lot the dolls were gone and he forgot about them.

She'd asked if he'd seen anyone else that morning or taken anything from the *casita*, but he just wagged his ponderous head like a friendly dog.

Frank waves a finger at the Pryce pictures she's propped against an empty flower vase.

"You were holding out on me," she tells the children. "You knew that all along. Naughty kids. How am I supposed to find the bad guy if you won't work with me?"

Frank has taken to animated conversations with the mute, smiling faces. In a more talkative person the habit might be amusing. Contrasted against Frank's natural reticence, the trait is ominous. Heedless of the portent, she circles the dining room tables, damaging as much of a fifth as she can before going to Gail's.

She's come to dread the hours of her leaving. Gail has become an image on the periphery of Frank's vision, an annoying shadow that will neither go away nor come into focus. Gail deserves more than her slightly besotted and grudging tolerance, but that's the best Frank can muster these days. She tells herself her apathy will pass, that someday she'll be able to see Gail clearly again and will remember why she fell in love with the doc. But for the moment, memory eludes her.

Frank sighs and glances at her wrist. She has an hour and twenty minutes left with her kids.

"Back to one perp," she tells them. "No problem. That's where we started this whole ride. So what have we got? One male, black. Age? I'm thinking older than your average bear. Anywhere from early thirties to mid-forties. Why, you say? Elementary, children."

For each point she makes Frank pops a finger from her fist.

"Your abduction—spontaneous as it may have been—was very well executed. It took nerve and finesse, not a combination usually found in your younger perps. The quality of the overall execution, from abduction through the assault to the dump, tells me this guy's either been thinking about this for a long time or he's done this before.

"Now, you might ask, if he's done this before, and he's a local boy like you insist, why don't we have similar cases popping up in the databases? Excellent question. To wit, I think he's also very smart. Not book smart, mind you, but savvy. Shrewd. He knows enough to strike well away from home.

"Which leads to an aside. I would expect him to be driving a high-mileage, dependable vehicle, something with a simple engine that he can make repairs on himself, because we know he's good with his hands, and he probably doesn't have a lot of money. He probably can't hold on to a job for long because of his stellar personality. He's anti-social and we can surmise he doesn't react well to stressors. Even if he has kept the same job for a while he's certainly not pro-motional material. But I digress."

Frank rattles the ice in her almost empty glass.

"He hits away from home. And I think he takes whatever victims happen along. Witness you two. Trevor, hate to say it, buddy, but you were just an afterthought. It was your sister he wanted. I'll bet he's got a considerable porn collection and spends a lot of time with it. Tides him over from strike to strike. Lots of helpless female/dom-inant male crap. He gets off on imagining himself in control of situ-ations, because in real life he's not. Like I said, low-income, poor people skills, and because he's smart, he probably knows he's missing out, that everyone's after him and that the world *owes* him.

"Look at the way he raped you, Ladeenia. Like he was *entitled* to you. We haven't found our boy because he's cunning. He's been around enough to know how the game is played, and he's smart enough to play without getting caught. He's learned a trick or two, and that comes with age."

93

Frank pauses long enough to pour Scotch over the vestigial ice cubes. The Pryce kids grin at her.

"So. Older black male. Some sort of skilled laborer. He's smart, so I think he needs to be challenged. He'll do something that requires some degree of training or experience. He might even be very good at it, but again, his personality will get in the way of advancement.

"How about his home life? Where does he live? Well, if he's employed he'll have a stable residence, but he can't be too selective about his job so he might have to travel a ways to get to it and still live in an area that his income dictates. Again, the need for a stable, reliable vehicle. It's probably well maintained, because we know he's organized and good with his hands. An older model in good shape. Probably something American, easy to work on, cheap parts. Probably doesn't trust foreign cars. Sorry. Again I digress."

She glances at her watch and drains the glass. Pours another inch from the bottle and prowls silently. Based on Ladeenia's multiple rapes, the perp is sexually adequate, so he could well be living with a female. But he took the kids somewhere private, a place probably not far from either the dump or the abduction site. So, if he is living with a woman, she wasn't home between 3:00 and 4:30 in the afternoon. Nor would she be expected to return as he had plenty of time with the children and kept their bodies presumably until he could dispose of them under cover of night.

The trace evidence on Ladeenia suggested she was attacked in a kitchen or a place where food is served, maybe a dining room. If the perp expected someone home sooner or later wouldn't he have sought more privacy?

"We know he's organized," Frank says to the kids. "He apparently had you both well in control. No defense marks on you, Ladeenia. Your nail scrapes came up negative. Nice, quiet little girl. He could have taken you wherever he wanted. So why'd he rape you in such a public space, where anyone could walk in and see him? He took a huge risk abducting you but that's really his only risk. Everything else he did was planned out. You two came to him somehow, didn't you? Not that I'm blaming you or saying you did anything bad, but somehow you crossed his path and he took advantage of that. Two kids walking alone in the late afternoon on a drizzly dark day . . .

"Maybe his stressor was a fight with the old lady, so he's sitting in his doorway, or in his garage, home alone, just thinking and drinking. He sees you, Ladeenia, and bam! He's gonna take what's his. Shit." It dawns on her. "I've been canvassing for a couple, and now we're back to a lone perp."

Frank decides she'll go back to the more cooperative people and ask questions based on the new profile.

"Okay. Whatever. We'll do what it takes. Back to your assault, Miss Ladeenia. The salient characteristic here? It wasn't personalized. He didn't cover your face, or blindfold you. Didn't bind you or perpetrate any kind of sadism or mutilation. The assault was completely impersonal, like you were as insignificant as a blow-up doll. You filled this guy's needs and then he dumped you like garbage. No anger, no remorse, just pure, narcissistic satisfaction. He was scratching an itch."

There was no indication the perp had a relationship with Ladeenia. He wouldn't care for or pretend to care for others. He would be self-absorbed and self-obsessed. His relationships were probably unsatisfying for both partners and Frank couldn't imagine them lasting long. If he'd been married it was probably for convenience. Maybe his women stayed because he had some money, a crib. He'd definitely cheat on them and he probably had a string of sexual contacts, most of them short-term because he probably had no motivation for a relationship other than sexual satisfaction. And more his own than his partner's.

Frank stops her relentless pacing long enough to make a few notes, then addresses the pictures.

"Got a little sidetracked there. Back to his chitty. Ah, and here's the crux of the thing. Get this. Assuming he takes good care of his ride, what better place for this guy to be—where he can see you two coming down the street and initiate contact with you—than in his driveway, or in his garage working on his car? It wasn't actually raining between three and four, just blustery. So he could have been outside, sees you coming, lures you into his garage somehow and bam—you're in the house. I like that."

She nurses the liquor, eyes closed, still for a moment. Not a family man, she thinks, so not a passenger vehicle. Sports cars take money and they're temperamental. They're flashy and compact. If this guy is a serious rapist, then he's going to spend a lot of time cruising around in his vehicle. He'll need space to spread out and feel comfortable. Nor would he appreciate a sports car's high visibility. And if he is a skilled laborer, he might have his own tools and need space for hauling them.

"Okay, boy and girl, here's my final answer. The tried-and-true criminal vehicle of choice, your average van. Or," Frank qualifies, "something roomy like a work truck with a shell. Maybe a used Blazer or Bronco. Something easy to fix. Plenty of space for parts, tools and the occasional unwitting victim. Not a conspicuous vehicle."

The alarm on Frank's wrist goes off.

"Nothing flashy or customized. Too expensive."

She tosses off the rest of the Black Label and jots a few notes.

"Love to stay," she says to the paper children, "but duty calls."

Chapter 20

After a peaceful enough night together, Gail calls Frank at work. "Guess what I've got?"

Frank almost says she hopes it's not an STD, but knows Gail wouldn't appreciate the crude humor. "The most beautiful legs in L.A.?"

"Just L.A.?"

"The planet," Frank allows.

"Tickets to *La Traviata*."

"Great. When?"

"Tonight! I won them on the radio driving in to work. Can you believe it?"

No, Frank thinks, she can't.

"Tonight?"

"Yeah, but don't worry. It's not opening night. You don't have to get dressed up. Your work clothes will be fine."

That's not what Frank's worried about, but the excitement in Gail's voice keeps her from admitting she'd rather cavity search a hope-to-die crackhead tonight than sit through two hours of Italian opera. Frank sighs without sound, asking where she should meet Gail and when.

The doc picks her up close to 5:30, the mandatory ten minutes late. She bursts radiantly through Frank's front door and for a shining second Frank loves her again. She warns herself not to be an asshole tonight.

Holding Gail close to her, Frank praises, "The most beautiful woman on the planet."

Gail beams and kisses her, but Frank's sincerity drains away like the tide around the pilings of the Santa Monica pier. She feels the suck of it leaving and tries to hold on, but she's left with only air. Gail picks this of all times to tell Frank, "I love you."

Even as she tells herself to just repeat the words, Frank is nodding, "I know. We better get going."

Later, Frank tells herself, in the bedroom's concealing darkness she'll tell Gail she loves her. Maybe then she'll feel the words. If she doesn't, maybe the night will hide her lie. They chat amiably during the return to downtown. Frank studies Gail's animated profile. She knows without reserve that Gail is playful, fun, sexy, bright—dozens of good adjectives—hence Frank's frustration at feeling nothing in kind but a low-level aversion.

The talk turns to their respective days. Frank returns the dutiful questions. When Gail asks if she got a chance to work on the Pryce case, Frank hesitates. It's a touchy subject.

"You still don't have any suspects?"

"Well, I didn't when I thought I was looking for a couple, but now that I'm back to a single perp again . . . I don't know. Probably not. There's a handful Noah kept looking at, but I haven't talked to them yet. They're not ringing any bells for me. One of them pimps really young girls." Ignoring Gail's shudder, Frank continues, "His grandmother lives on the same block where the bodies were found and she was gone all afternoon. The house was empty and the grandson had a key. Came and went as he pleased. He's got weak alibis for the time period, but there's no hard evidence against him. Ladeenia's personal effects—"

"Ladeenia?"

"Yeah. She's the girl. Her—"

"Since when are you on a first-name basis with your victims?"

Frank checks a sigh. "Is there a point to this line of questioning?"

"You don't usually refer to your victims by their first names. It sounds so personal."

Not willing to follow where she thinks Gail is going, Frank slogs on, "So all the physical evidence got lost somewhere at SID."

"You don't say."

Lost evidence is not uncommon in a bureaucracy the size of the LAPD, but Gail's sarcasm still rankles. Frank jabs back, "There's no DNA to match to these guys because the sperm was too degraded by the time the coroner got around to autopsying her. Second guy's down in Calipatria, violent sexual predator. Same for him. Weak alibi, no evidence, tight story. The best of the three raped a thirteen-year-old at knifepoint but was apparently up north when the kid—" Frank catches herself. "When the case went down. There's a handful of guys in the area with priors, but they've never developed into viable suspects."

"Let me see if I've got this straight. You're working a—how old is this case?"

"Six years."

"Okay. You're working a six-year-old case, with no physical evidence, no suspects and no witnesses. And you expect to clear this how?"

"Through dint of my superior investigative acumen."

Gail shoots an eyebrow up. "Wow. I think you've been hanging around me too long."

"Maybe so, Shakespeare."

Frank used to call Gail that when they first started dating, when

Gail hid her nervousness behind big words and formal speech. Now the name softens her and Gail asks, "So what do you think happened to all your evidence?"

"No clue."

Frank explains that the blanket the kids were found under, their clothing and the tape on their bodies all were collected by the coroner investigator, as they should have been. Detectives don't usually handle the transfer of evidence from the coroner's office to the SID facility but in this case Noah had signed out the physical evidence and personally delivered it to William Kastanaphoulas at Piper Tech. Because of SID's backlog and the Pryce case's low priority, it took four months, with constant nagging on Noah's part, for Kastanaphoulas to analyze the material.

When Noah finally got the message from SID that the evidence had been processed he'd raced to Ramirez Street, only to be told that Kastanaphoulas had gone to Oklahoma for two weeks. Noah talked to the Trace Evidence supervisor who authorized another criminalist to sign out Noah's package. Noah waited while she went to get it, only to be horrified when she couldn't find the evidence. She found copies of the lab reports and turned those over to him, but the blanket, clothing and tape weren't anywhere. Noah had looked with her. They checked every log and record. They talked to each person associated with the case. They searched Kastanaphoulas's work area. But the evidence had vanished.

Frank had managed to calm Noah by reasoning that at least he had the lab reports to work with and that Kastanaphoulas would probably be able to lay his hands on the material as soon as he got back from Oklahoma. Noah had consoled himself with the slim laboratory findings, fruitlessly tracking trace fibers back to the Pryce home. The fibers he couldn't track were so common as to be useless.

On the morning of Kastanaphoulas's return, Noah had cornered the criminalist before he could pour his first cup of coffee. Kastanaphoulas explained that he'd packaged the material and left Noah the message to pick it up. That was a week before he'd left town. He remembered being surprised, and a little pissed, that for all his hurry Noah still hadn't collected the evidence by the time he'd left for Oklahoma. Because the evidence was labeled with Noah's name and the Figueroa address, Kastanaphoulas's best guess was that the evidence had been mistakenly delivered to the station. Noah had ransacked Figueroa's Property Room and then gone on a tear through the Property Division's warehouse, but all for naught. The evidence never materialized.

"How frustrating."

"Whatever." Frank shrugs. "It happens. It was more frustrating for Noah than me. It drove him hard. I wish I'd have helped him with it before he—" And again Frank cuts herself off. "I never had the time," she says out the window.

"And now it's a one-woman crusade."

Frank slings the doc a glance. "I don't know that I'd say that."

Gail doesn't comment, asking only where Frank wants to eat.

"Ladies' choice," Frank answers. Her thoughts flee to the Pryce case. While Gail chats about her mother, Frank tries to figure when she can finagle interviews of Noah's suspects into her schedule.

Chapter 21

"World owes me a living," Frank says to her glass. Her ass may be planted on her couch but her head isn't. Idly going over the Pryce photographs, hoping a clue might kick loose, she's drifted into the perp's head. She imagines him different places just before he sees the kids.

It's Ladeenia he sees first. Something about her pulls at him. Her smallness and vulnerability. He feels strong just watching her. The boy walks beside his sister. The children approach him, unsuspecting. This feeds his ego. An idea pops into his head and he looks around the neighborhood. No one sits outside; it's too cold. Shades are pulled and windows are rain-spotted. The kids come closer, still not alarmed, and he hides his excitement. Their thin voices are muted by the damp air. He focuses on the girl. He likes to watch her walk. She's so little. So fine. The boy has almost disappeared from his vision. He watches them approach and his idea blossoms like a flower from hell.

The unnamable longing that's never as far from him as his shadow evaporates in a rush of excitement. His brain is on fire, but you wouldn't know it to look at him. The children don't sense it. They're closer now. Closer. Here. Looking at him. Maybe they know him, maybe they've seen him before. None of that matters now. Nothing matters. Just getting her into the house, that's all that matters. Quiet. No fuss. Oh, please just come with me. Yes, and they do.

Frank's voice is spidery. "How do I do it? Come see my puppy? Come in? Hurry, rain's coming. Want a cookie, a cupcake? Would you like to meet my little girl? She's sick, she inside. Come on in."

And then they're in, and he locks the door and the adrenaline's shooting through him like he's doing eightballs. He wants to get the boy out of the way. He's a distraction. All he can think about is the girl. He's got her. He's in control and his cock leaps like a rabbit. It gets harder as he holds the boy so he can't scream. In a quiet voice he warns her not to scream either or he'll hurt the boy. He's smart. He knows the girl's older than the boy and responsible for him. She won't want to get a whipping, so she watches silently as he gropes in a drawer and binds the boy in tape.

Now he's so hard he can't stand it. He thinks he's gonna rupture if he doesn't get inside her so he takes her right there. Right against the table. Doesn't realize he's imbedding food grains into her bared bottom and the backs of her hands and he's barely in her before he comes and comes and comes. The climax leaves him spent, and while he gets his breath back he contemplates his find. No way he's turning her loose. Uh-uh. Not yet. He breathes heavily. He doesn't talk to either child, except for an occasional command. He eyes the girl crumpled under the table. She cries with muted sobs, too terrified to make noise. The boy's eyes bulge over his taped mouth. He doesn't know what's going on.

Frank's left hand pats for the fifth on the floor. Her fingers can't find it. Annoyed, she pins the folder on her chest with her right hand and rolls onto her shoulder to retrieve the bottle. She pours at an awkward angle and drops of Scotch spill onto the carpet. She frowns more at the waste than the mess, even though she's taken to bringing Mr. Walker home by the case. She fluffs the booze into the carpet pile and settles back.

"Where were we?" she asks the books lining the wall. "Oh, yeah."

Watching the girl. He smokes while he watches and is sated for a moment. But the more he revels in his pleasure, the more he wants to relive it. His cock thickens as he finishes his cigarette. Does he touch her? Does the fresh skin excite him?

"No," Frank says against her glass. He's not tripping on sex with a little girl. He's tripping on the power, the command. Totally dominating the situation. Even the little boy he barely notices fuels his desire. He is in complete and total control and it's like being God. So he takes her again. Rougher this time, longer. And from behind.

Ladeenia's anal trauma was extensive, leading Frank to think this was the second, less impulsive assault. He maintained his erection longer and did more damage. He takes her against the stove this time, or the counter, and maybe this is where she burns her thumb, on a burner or coffeepot. Again he doesn't notice. Or care. She means nothing to him. Nothing. All he knows is that when he's inside her it's quiet in his head. For a moment that seems to stretch into infinity, the squirming in his brain is stilled.

Frank's mouth twists humorlessly. She understands the longing for surcease. Her glass is empty and she pours again, meticulously. Photographs from the Pryce case drop from the folder on her chest. They surround her like leaves from a wintry oak. Except for the two she clutches in her hand, as if in cadaveric spasm.

One is a long-shot of the street where the Pryce kids were found. Cars line both sides of the road, houses opposite the curbs. The other picture is a shot of the west end of the street. More cars, a truck with a camper, a couple work trucks, more houses. Nothing significant. Nothing that jumps out shouting, "Hey, look at me!"

Frank's hand drops as she passes out. It is finally quiet in her head.

Until she bolts from the couch, immediately aware of her surroundings and the sick whomping in her head. The fifth that was full last night is almost empty at her feet.

Frank wonders how this has happened again. She'd sworn herself to two drinks, max. How the fuck did she down most of a bottle? She remembers carrying it in here and pouring a generous nightcap, putting some CDs in, and that's about it. The effort of plumbing her lost evening is curtailed by a lurch in her gut. Frank barely makes it to the kitchen sink. She pukes until she's empty, but her stomach still contracts reflexively. Frank gulps for air in between the huge, choking spasms. When she's finally able to straighten up she looks at her watch. 5:25. She has barely half an hour to get to work. Her stomach folds in on itself, forcing Frank back over the sink. She brings up nothing but hard air.

Forty-five minutes later—pale, sore and shaky—Frank starts the morning brief. Johnnie doesn't look much better and Frank is disgusted. She *swears* she will cut back.

Chapter 22

Using existing information, Frank has constructed a victimology of the Pryce kids. She's going over it again in her office, trying to find something she may have missed the first time. Noah had talked to the parents, surviving siblings, neighbors, friends and teachers, even their bus driver. He'd cross-checked each kid's personality, habits, hobbies, friends and routines. His notes on them alone took up half a binder.

The victims are not prostitutes, bangers or drug dealers, but they did live in a fairly high-crime area. They didn't frequent rough bars or rock houses, but both places abound in the area. The vics were young and alone. That alone put them at risk for being victims. Frank puts her pad down and considers the shoebox on her desk. She still hasn't listened to the interview tapes. She'll have to sometime but is still willing to settle for Noah's written notes. She parses his initial interview with Mr. and Mrs. Pryce. It's bare facts, nothing not in the reports.

Curiosity harps at Frank and she fingers through the tapes. Some are starred. She pulls one of these, reading a label marked *Sharon Ferris*.

"Oh, for Christ's sake." She almost knocks her chair over as she jumps up. "Just get it the fuck over with."

She puts the tape in her boom box, stabbing the play button. After the introductory hiss, Noah's voice announces he's investigating the death of two children that lived on Raymond Street. Frank cuts it off. Noah's voice slices like a sword fresh from the forge. Her pain morphs into rage and she wants to break something. The boom box. Just pick it up and slam it down until it's in two-inch pieces. She imagines the satisfaction of slamming the box over and over on the edge of her desk, the noise and splintering and the shock of it in her hands. She thinks about this instead of Noah and the rage ebbs.

Frank stands straight over the stereo. She stares at the box and drags in a leveling breath. After a moment she says, "Okay. Let's try again."

"*What were you doing that afternoon?*"

"*I can't say for sure.*"

"*Take your time. I know it was a while ago. I can't even remember what I had for dinner last night.*" Noah's standard line. She can see the big, friendly grin attached to it.

"*I don't know nothing about that afternoon. Just like any other I guess.*"

"*What do you usually do in the afternoon?*"

Frank hears the shrug in her voice as the woman answers, "*Watch Oprah, I guess. Get dinner ready.*"

"*For the record, who else lives here with you?*"

"*My two boys and my husband.*"

Noah asks for everyone's names and she tells him.

"*How old are your boys?*"

"*James is nineteen, Levon's seventeen.*"

"*Must take a while to make dinner.*" Again Noah's grin comes through the tape recorder and Frank almost turns it off. "*Who was home with you that afternoon?*"

The tape hisses, picks up shuffling noises.

"Kevin'd be working and the boys wasn't home yet. I don't know where they was at, but they wasn't with me."

"Where does your husband work?"

Frank pauses the tape to hunt through the interview folders. That Noah doesn't follow up on the boy's whereabouts tells her he's already placed them during the critical time frame. His notes on Levon indicate he and James were doing blunts and videos at a friend's house. Satisfied, she continues the tape.

"Over to Grand Tire, off 'n Hoover."

She hears more shifting, then Noah asks, *"Can you recall anything unusual about that day?"* There's no answer and Noah prompts, *"Did you notice anyone unfamiliar outside or hear any funny noises you couldn't place?"*

"No. Nothing I recollect."

"Mrs. Ferris, are you sure there wasn't anyone else home with you that day?"

More shifting, then over-bright, the woman says, *"I forgot. My brother was visitin'."*

Consulting the notes, Frank reads that the interview was done as a follow-up to identifying the vehicles photographed within the vicinity of the dumpsite. Noah's disembodied voice asks where the brother was visiting from.

"From up north. Up to Bakersfield, where our folks live."

"Where was he that afternoon?"

"Right here with me. He ain't never far from the kitchen when I'm in it. He's always pestering me something awful about when's the next meal and what's it gonna be. Lord, that man is worse than both my boys. You'd think he had a worm the way he eats."

"How much of the day did he spend here with you?"

"All of it, as I recollect. We went to the Ralph's in the morning and I made him bring the groceries in, then I fixed him lunch and we watched TV and played Mexican Train until suppertime."

"What's Mexican Train?"

"Dominoes. I recollect it was rainy and I made a stew. I thought it would last Kevin for lunch next day, but didn't Antoine eat it right up!"

"Dang! You must be a pretty fair cook."

"I know my way aroun' a kitchen."

"I'm jealous, Mrs. Ferris."

Frank hears the grin again and recalls Noah's prodigious appetite. He was always hungry, always noshing on something and never gaining a pound. He got written up in his rookie year because he waited for his order at the drive-through before responding to a Code 2 burglary.

Frank hits the stop button. She can't do this. She needs a drink. Being on call, she can't get ripped, but by-fucking-Christ she can at least get a sweet buzz on. Drinking on call is a gross violation. One Frank often overlooks for a drink or two. Tonight she needs more than a drink or two and considers calling Fubar.

"Fuck it," she declares. "End of watch."

She grabs her jacket, willing to take the chance that she doesn't get called out.

But it's a bad bet. Just as she's oiled herself into bed after *Nightline*, the phone rings. The watch commander calls her out to a domestic with an ugly ending.

Frank dresses while assessing her condition. She's tired but fairly clearheaded. She rinses with Scope and runs a little soap through her hair, hoping the combined scents will camouflage the ethanol seeping from her pores.

"Not good," she reprimands the Frank in the mirror. Her eyes are bloodshot, but she justifies, "What do you expect for the middle of the night." Then, "Still, girlie-girl. Tail's startin' to wag the dog."

Frank packs her ID, gun, cuffs, wallet, notebook and change. Stuffing a stray latex glove into her jacket pocket, she takes off into the night that never really gets dark in Los Angeles. She drives fast, with the windows down, and the cool air makes her feel sober. She's *got* to make a limit to her drinking and stick to it, especially on week-nights and call duty. Though exhausted, she feels better by the time she gets to the scene.

Until Jill storms up to her, firing off, "Johnnie's pasted."

She follows her detective into an apartment with a lot of crying kids. The battered body of a female Hispanic lies on the kitchen floor. Johnnie stands next to her making a peanut butter and jelly sandwich. When he sees Frank he grins, "Hey, Freek! You hungry?"

She steps to him and puts out her hand. "Give me your weapon and your ID."

Johnnie laughs. "What for?"

"You're suspended."

"What for? For making a sandwich? I'm hungry. It was sitting right here."

"You're drunk, Johnnie. Turn 'em over."

Certain Frank's bluffing, he says, "Whoa, lighten up, ol' Freek. I'm not drunk."

He tries wrapping a beefy limb around her shoulder, but Frank knocks it away.

"Hey, come on," he says, startled, swaying gently.

Frank motions two of the uniforms but Johnnie backs away from them.

"Quit it. You can't do this to me."

"Watch me." She advances on Johnnie and the uniforms follow her lead.

He bellows, "Fuck you, Frank. Who the fuck you think you are? Your shit don't stink? How many times you come on lately smelling like a fuckin' barroom, huh?"

The uniforms have stopped. Jill and the onlookers glance between Johnnie and Frank.

"Who'za one always closing the Alibi with me, ripped to the tits? And on call too, huh? How many you had tonight? Everyone knows you been sluggin' 'em back since—"

Later she will realize it was a suicidal move, but Frank doesn't have the luxury of hindsight as her fist connects under Johnnie's chin. The blow staggers him, but the following left to his temple wakes him to murder. Frank steps out of Johnnie's first swing but can't avoid the second. It glances off her shoulder and slows her long enough for his third punch to land on her jaw. Frank's head snaps 180 degrees and she thinks of Trevor Pryce as the lights go out.

Chapter 23

"What in God's name were you thinking?"

Slumped on Gail's couch, Frank mumbles that if she were thinking she obviously wouldn't have swung at a man with over a hundred pounds on her.

Gail only glares.

Frank is tired. Foubarelle, the deputy chief, the IAD rats, even the drug-recognition expert who took Johnnie's urine sample (Frank was ordered to give hers, almost as an afterthought, well past dawn), they've all pointed out how stupid that was. She doesn't need to be reminded, thank you very much. She just wants to get some sleep, but Gail won't let it go.

Frank's jaw feels like it's packed with wet cement. She tries to minimize movement inside her mouth as she asks, "Shouldn't you be at work?"

"You know, I *should*. But my girlfriend picked a fight with a three-hundred-pound subordinate last night and I'm kind of curious why."

"Got a lot on my mind. Johnnie just hit a nerve and I reacted poorly. End of story."

"End of story."

Gail is pacing back and forth in front of the couch. The hypnotic motion makes Frank sleepy, but Gail's precarious balance on the edge of fury keeps Frank wary.

The doc grits out, "I'm trying to be sensitive here, Frank. I know you're under a lot of pressure. Granted, most of it is self-imposed, but I'm trying to overlook that. I'm giving you the benefit of the doubt, that you know the best way to work this out for yourself, but frankly, I'm losing patience. It's been almost four months, Frank. Four months in which you have done nothing but obsess about a six-year-old case and drink yourself comatose. I feel more inconsequential in your life than that sofa you're sitting on. Now you breeze in at eight in the morning and tell me you've been suspended for decking one of your own men, and I'm just supposed to take this in stride too?"

Frank doesn't need this. She feels stupid enough. Knowing Gail would find out sooner or later, Frank had decided she'd rather tell the doc herself. It was as dumb to stop by Gail's as it was to swing on Johnnie. Frank reckons she's on a dumb streak.

Pulling herself from the couch's warm embrace, she tells Gail, "I don't care what you do with it."

Gail half barks, half laughs, "Oh, don't even think about leaving, Frank. *Don't* even think about it."

Frank turns, as cold as the backup piece she clips onto her belt. "Why stay? I made a mistake coming here. Shouldn't compound it."

Gail looks like she's been bitch-slapped but answers, "Because good or bad, we're in this together, Frank, and that's how we'll work it out. Together. We can't do that if you keep running away."

"There's nothing to work out, Gail. That's my whole point. And you keep insisting there is."

"Is that really the way you feel?"

"It really is."

Gail's fury is instantly quenched by tears. Guilt tries to pierce Frank's armor but fails. She pats her pockets, making sure she has her keys. It'd be embarrassing to slam out and have to come back for them.

"Frank?"

When Frank meets her eyes, Gail says, "If you walk out that door, don't bother coming back."

Frank pauses, squaring her shoulders. It's a big threat and she gauges Gail's sincerity. She looks serious enough, and probably has every right to an ultimatum, but Frank doesn't give a shit. That's really the bottom line. She just doesn't fucking care.

"Sorry," she says, and slips out the door.

Chapter 24

The new sun is fresh and pretty. When Frank gets home she remains in her car, soaking in it. Her anger has cooled to remorse, and the morning's clarity emphasizes how brilliantly she's erred. She tells herself that yes, Johnnie was drunk, and yes, he would have been suspended anyway, but none of that negates the fact that she'd been drinking too. Despite his unjustifiable method of delivery, Johnnie's message was dead-bang true. Frank had swung because she didn't want to hear she was just like him.

Dropping head into hand, she massages her eyebrows while rats chew at her guts.

"Christ on a fucking pony." She's acting as badly as Briggs, a man who needs professional help. A man who can't control his drinking.

This last is unacceptable. She *can* control her drinking. She's just been under a lot of pressure lately and hasn't policed herself closely enough. She is *not* like Briggs, who barely has the discipline to bathe himself. She can control her drinking and she will. She's just gotten sloppy. Lazy. She'll go that far in comparing herself to Johnnie. But no further.

Frank is beyond exhaustion. She tips her head toward the headrest and is almost asleep before it gets there.

"Come on," she rouses herself. "Discipline. Word for the day."

Despite how odd it feels to slide between sheets at nine in the morning, Frank is soon deeply under. She sleeps through to sunset. Her jaw still hurts when she wakes up but she likes the pain. It distracts her from anything deeper while reminding her what an asshole she was. She turns the volume on the phone back up and listens to six messages, hopeful that one is from Gail. Jill, the lab, Bobby, a clerk in admin, Darcy and Fubar. The captain tells her she's to report back to work on Monday. Frank won't admit relief over the last call, or disappointment that Gail's not on the machine.

She works up a hard sweat in the gym, then showers and returns phone calls. Jill backed her following the incident, stating that Johnnie was drunk and belligerent. When IA asked if Frank had been defending herself, Jill hadn't hesitated to say yes, despite every other witness stating that Frank had swung first. She calls Jill, admitting that she was wrong, that Johnnie got her goat and she lost it. Having worked with him, Jill can empathize. Having worked with Frank, Jill's grateful Johnnie's the one she finally chose to blow up on.

That evening, Frank drinks moderately, by her standards, refilling her tumbler only once. Saturday morning she is surprised that she went to bed early and slept through the night. She feels good outside, but dirty inside. At noon she calls Johnnie. He sounds awful.

"How you doin'?" she asks.

"All right, I guess."

After a beat, she confides, "Sorry about the other night."

"Fuck, I don't even remember it."

"Remember getting called out?"

"Sort of. I remember getting dressed and driving. That's kind of where I lose it."

116

Frank is relieved. There's no need for her to come clean. Johnnie doesn't remember a thing. He has been suspended, pending further review after completion of a mandatory 30-day in-house treatment program. She listens to his ensuing alcoholic admissions like a priest. A dirty priest. When he is done, she apologizes for not helping him sooner. She's known he's had problems and she's hoped they'd go away.

"Me too." He chokes out a laugh.

"It was hard for me to call you on your shit, 'cause it meant calling me on my own. You were right, you know. You accused me of drinking too much, and I have been. I gotta take care of that."

"Yeah, before you get a thirty-day rehab. Man, I don't want to go, Frank. Can't you get me out of it?"

"No can do, buddy. You gotta take this bullet."

"Fuck," he moans and Frank's heart aches for him. Johnnie's a pain in the ass, but he's her pain in the ass. And like it or not, he's become her conscience.

"Your desk'll be waiting for you when you get back, big man. It's gonna be all right."

"Yeah. Okay," he agrees, sounding unconvinced.

Frank hangs up feeling worse for her self-serving noblesse oblige. Granted, she hadn't been as hammered as he was, but probably the only thing keeping her from a bunk next to Johnnie's was that her BAC had dissipated by the time the brass thought to collect her urine sample.

She goes cold turkey that afternoon and starts listening to the Pryce tapes. She's aware that she's waiting for the phone to ring. But Gail doesn't call. And she still hasn't called when Frank gets home from work on Monday night. Confident she can control her drinking because she was sober yesterday and only had two drinks on Saturday, she heads straight for the Scotch. She savors the liquor's torch as it lights up her belly.

Sipping slowly, making the glass last, she debates the lightless answering machine. It was Gail's ultimatum, she decides, so Gail will have to break it. If she doesn't, maybe that's just as well. Frank would be the first to admit that she's been awful company lately.

Sliding a frozen dinner into the oven, she decides the day went pretty well, considering. The first thing she did after clipping her Beretta and ID back on was to apologize to the rest of the crew. What she did was unprofessional and made the whole department look bad. Yeah, she's been stressed, but so has everyone so that's no excuse. The incident was being recommended to the Board of Review and Frank agreed to abide by whatever actions the BOR saw fit to impose.

The rest of the day was routine. Despite the disruption to her crime scene Jill had nailed the suspect in the domestic and brought him in. Frank had to go out to the range for her monthly qualification and Darcy rode with her. In between reloads, he casually reminded Frank that he didn't drink anymore and that he might be able to help with Johnnie, or whatever. Reflecting on the implication of "or whatever," Frank thanked him and let the comment pass.

Frank only has a quarter-inch of booze left in her glass and it's barely four o'clock. She has to get through the rest of the night with just one more drink. But, she allows, she can have a glass of wine before dinner and another with dinner, then the second half-tumbler of Scotch for dessert. That's reasonable enough, she decides, and puts her glass down to save the last swallow.

She walks around the house, restless. She wishes she could talk to Noah. Which reminds her that Tracey called last week. She'd left a message asking where Frank has been, when are they going to see her again? Frank hasn't returned the call yet. She feels guilty as hell but Trace and the kids are bleeding raw reminders. She can't face them right now. She needs to forget for a while. Forget everything. Noah, Gail, Johnnie—all of them. Just get everybody out of her head. The only way she knows to do that is to work. And drink.

Downing the last sip of Scotch, Frank pours a glass of wine. She starts to carry it into the shower with her but then leaves it on the counter.

"Pacing," she tells herself. "Just slow it down."

She ignores the clamoring from heart, bone and fingertips, all telling her to guzzle the waiting drink and chase it with a hundred more. Walking away from the glass is harder than facing open fire and leaves Frank trembling almost as badly.

Chapter 25

Noah talks through her stereo. He sounds relaxed, like he's talking smack with his dawgs. It hurts to hear his voice, but she concentrates on Reginald McNabb's. He and Noah joke and Frank winces when Noah laughs. She plays the tape through, hunting for inconsistencies that aren't there. Or that she can't hear.

She's drinking beer tonight instead of the hard stuff. When she gets up to play a new tape, she opens another bottle. Noah dictates the date, time and place of the interview. He introduces himself and, for the record, the woman he is talking to. She's the last of the hookers McNabb talked to the night of the murders. After a few minutes of bio background Noah asks her where she was that night.

"Where I always am. Corner of Florence and Vermont."

"Was it a busy night?"

"Hell, no! It was freezing. Wasn't nobody out."

"Did you have any tricks that night?"

"Uh-uh. Not a one. I was fixin' a go home, and that's when Reg rolled on me. I told him I was freezin' my ass off for nothing and all he was gonna get from me that night was fuckin' pneumonia. He told me he'd be back in a hour and that if I wasn't there I'd better have some cash for him in the mornin'."

Frank hears her suck on a cigarette.

"What happened then?"

"He went on and I stayed. Didn't get no fuckin' trick and that pimp nigger never did roll back. Probably went home to his warm bed and slappin' guts."

"Was that the last time you saw him that night?" She must have nodded because Noah says, *"I need a verbal response, Tina."*

"Yeah. That was the last time."

"What sort of mood was he in the last time you saw him?"

"Like always. Like the lyin' snake he is, somewhere's between charmin' and deadly."

Not the attitude Frank would expect from a man who'd just tossed, or still had to toss, two dead kids. The more Frank hears, the more she discounts McNabb as a primary suspect. She has a moment of regret, guilt even, that she didn't help Noah sooner and harder. She thinks of all the energy and emotion he spent running down dead ends.

On paper McNabb looks like a logical suspect, but his story holds up well after at least three lengthy interrogations. So do the testimonies of the girls, his homes and the bartender. Second, of the little physical evidence there was, none pointed to McNabb. Third, McNabb fits neither her profile nor the FBI's, although the latter was submitted when it was believed the suspect had positioned the bodies. Frank has since resubmitted the case data and is anxious to see if VICAP's new profile corresponds to hers. At any rate, barring a confession or a witness stepping forward, she has nothing on McNabb to present to a grand jury.

But like Noah, she will beat this horse to death. After a late lunch the next day, Frank heads back to Raymond Street. She hopes to find

McNabb's grandmother home and is pleased when the old lady answers her knock. After Frank introduces herself, Mrs. McNabb whispers that she has some friends visiting. Frank promises this won't take long. The old lady is peeved but invites her in.

"I'll just be a minute," she tells her friends as she and Frank pass the living room. Two old women stare at Frank, then start whispering as she passes from sight. Mrs. McNabb pulls a chair almost as tall as she is from the kitchen table. She sits but doesn't offer Frank a seat.

"Mrs. McNabb, you spent a lot of time talking to my partner, Detective Jantzen, about your grandson Reginald and his possible involvement in the deaths of Ladeenia and Trevor Pryce."

The old lady bobs her head so violently Frank half expects it to snap off and roll around on the kitchen floor. She continues with her questions, confirming answers she already has, and retesting the strength of Mrs. McNabb's testimony. At length Mrs. McNabb rises on tiny feet, complaining, "Lieutenant, my friends are out there waiting on me and the God's honest truth is I am just *tired* of all these suggestions that my grandson is a petit four."

"A petit four." Frank blinks.

"Yes," she says with heat, "or whatever you call those child molesters."

"Mrs. McNabb, I'm certainly not implying that Reginald is a petit four, but he may have gotten into a situation he didn't anticipate. I've talked with Reginald. He's a bright boy, and I think at heart he means well, but sometimes accidents happen. Things get out of hand and suddenly we've made a mess we're not sure how to clean up. The normal thing is to panic and run, try to hide our tracks. That's all I'm saying. And to be honest, from the outside looking in, your grandson looks like a pretty good suspect. Whether he was involved or not, that's what it looks like."

The old lady appears calmed by the lies. Good cops develop a wonderful sense of timing, and Frank's tells her she's pushed far enough today. Mrs. McNabb makes sure to see her out, asking at the door, "Where'd that young detective go? I liked him a lot better."

"I liked him a lot better too," Frank admits. "But he's off the case. You're stuck with me now."

"He off 'cause he didn't solve it?"

It's good for the old lady to believe the case is that important so Frank nods.

Alone in the car, she allows a chuckle. Gail will love Mrs. McNabb's petit four/pedophile malapropism. Her humor fades when she remembers she won't be seeing Gail. Or talking to her. Or Noah, either. There's no one to tell. The extraordinary depth of her isolation stuns Frank, snatching her breath away.

"Christ."

She needs a drink. It's the only thing she knows to do to ease the crush in her chest. She races toward the Alibi, feeling better just thinking about the relief a drink will bring. Frank's certain this is not a good solution but equally certain she doesn't have a better one. Jammed up in traffic on Manchester, she has time to see a familiar face pass along the sidewalk. Frank idles up to a woman too nicely dressed for the 'hood and too large-boned to be a woman.

"Hey. Buy you a drink, miss?"

"Officer Frank," she gushes in a breathy voice. "Whatever you want it's gonna cost you more than a drink."

"Don't I know it."

Frank tips her head toward the seat next to her. Miss Cleo minces around the grill, smoothing her skirt as she settles beside Frank.

"You can't drive better than this on your salary?"

"What's wrong with this?" Frank asks.

"It's *old*, what's wrong with it. Look like something my grandma'd drive." Miss Cleo sniffs.

She's a classy hooker, but there aren't that many classy bars in South Central. The Sizzler's close and clean. Two 10-7 uniforms snicker as Frank and Miss Cleo take a table. Miss Cleo orders red wine, removing the white gloves that cover her telltale wrist bones. An artfully tied scarf conceals the large Adam's apple, and Miss Cleo remains the image of a sophisticated lady.

"Being careful out there?" Frank asks.

The ageless transvestite flashes a snowy smile. "I'm here, aren't I?"

Frank pulls pictures from her briefcase, sliding them across the table. "You know any of these guys?"

The drinks come and Frank finishes half her beer before Miss Cleo's first sip. She studies pictures of Noah's three suspects but at last shakes her head. Feathers wave from the cloche over her ironed bangs.

"What'd they do?"

"Detective Jantzen ever talk to you—"

"Oh, I heard he passed. I'm so sorry about that. He was a lovely man."

Frank responds with one nod. "He ever talk to you about a case he had a while back? Two kids dumped in a lot near Raymond Street. Strangled." Trevor's broken neck is still a holdback.

Miss Cleo's fine features draw together in concentration. "It seems like it. Yes, I think so. That've been about four, five years ago, hmm?"

"Six. This guy, Reginald McNabb"—she taps his picture—"is a pimp. He lives over to Raymond. Keeps a stable of really young girls. Don't think he has one over sixteen. He likes it front and back. That's how the little girl was done. This guy, Charles Floyd, he's just a hustler. I want to know what the word is on him. And this guy, name's Willie Coleman. He likes kids. Down in Calipatria right now, serving a dime on a child molest. "

The feathers bounce in understanding. Frank finishes her beer, already wanting another. She lays two twenties on the table.

Miss Cleo is surprised. "You don't usually pay in advance."

"I don't usually care this much. Can I give you a ride somewhere?"

Chapter 26

At the coffeepot next morning, she asks Bobby, "How goes it, Picasso?"

Hunching his broad shoulders, he answers in his sweet voice, "Weird. It goes weird."

"How so?"

"I don't know. Just feels weird without Noah, and Johnnie gone now too."

"Yeah. I know."

They both look over the squad room. Jill's typing and Lewis is on the phone.

"How goes it with you?" Bobby asks over the rim of his cup.

She thinks for a moment, then confides, "You're the art major. You'll appreciate this. You know Munch's *The Scream*? The skinny woman with her mouth open like an *O*?"

"Yeah." Bobby nods.

Heading toward her office, Frank says over her shoulder, "It goes like that."

Unable to stand the confining squad room, twenty minutes later Frank checks out a slickback and drives to McNabb's crib.

Noah had dragged Reginald McNabb down to the station no less than three times, and each time his testimony was consistent. McNabb was at the Cozy Corner from about 2:30 to 4:00 on that Friday afternoon. Ladeenia and Trevor left their house around 3:30. According to McNabb, there was no one to kick it with at the bar, so he left. He cruised around looking for his homes, couldn't find any. He stopped at the B & O for cigarettes. He got a Quick Pick and five scratchers. None of the dated tickets were winners and he'd thrown them out. The owner of the store didn't remember him. He doesn't have a substantial alibi until he appears at Jackson's Bar at almost 6:00. The bartender and three homes back his story. He has two Seven-and-Sevens then goes out to make sure his hos are getting ready for work. The girls Noah talked to support the timing. Reginald spends the better part of the night hustling. Christmas is coming and he needs bank. His girl Tina is the last to see him that night, around 11:30.

The morning is still young when Frank pulls up to McNabb's. A bronze Camry, tricked out with gold rims and personalized plates reading BIGPMPN, announces he is home. This pleases Frank. The best time to trip a suspect up is when they've just been pounded out of bed. Frank flashes ID at a woman behind the cracked door.

"What you want him for?"

"Wanna talk to him."

Seeing Frank's alone, the woman admits her. She starts to walk away but Frank catches her arm.

"He asleep?"

"He was till you started banging on the door."

"Where?"

The woman is dubious but points down a hall with three open doors.

"On the right or left?"

"Left. The second one."

Frank walks into a dim room. Reginald McNabb sleeps on his belly, hugging a pillow. Even in bed he is decked out in emeralds and ice. A sheet covers him from half his ass down. Frank loves this. She sits next to him, tickling his back with her badge. He swats at it, slurring into the pillow, "Keesh, wha' you doin'?"

Frank holds a finger in front of her lips, glancing at a nervous Keesh in the doorway. Frank trails the badge over the small of McNabb's back and he rolls over in a flurry. His speed surprises Frank, but not as much as she's surprised him.

He grabs the sheets, spitting, "Who the fuck are you?" even though she's held her badge up for him.

"Lieutenant Franco. Homicide. Where were you the night Ladeenia Pryce was killed?"

"*What?*"

She repeats the question.

"Bitch, what the fuck you *talkin'* about? Comin' into my house like this! Wakin' me up in my bed. I'ma slap a harassment suit on you's what I'ma do. You got a warrant?"

"Don't need one. Keesh let me in. Where were you the night Ladeenia Pryce was killed?"

"Keesha, you one stupid bitch, you know that? I do not fuckin' believe this," he moans. "Why you people still all over me 'bout them kids?"

"Where were you the—"

"I was the same fuckin' place I was the last time you five-oh motherfuckers axed me! Keesha! Why you let this bitch in here?"

Keesha only answers with wider eyes.

"Where were you the night Ladeenia Pryce was killed?"

"Same fuckin' place, a'ight! To the Cozy Corner, then Jackson's, a'ight! It's the same fuckin' story. It ain't changed. Don't be puttin' it on me 'cause you stupid motherfuckin' one-times can't find your killuh."

"Put some clothes on." Frank stands. "Could you make us some coffee, Keesha?"

"What I look like, your fuckin' housemaid?"

McNabb barks, "Bitch, make the goddamned coffee."

Frank waits in the sparsely furnished living room, McNabb's strewn clothing the only decoration. She studies a high-end entertainment system until he appears in jeans and a T-shirt.

"Nice works," she says. "Probably costs more than I make in half a year."

"Yeah." He snorts. " 'Cause you the only honest cop left in America, right?"

"Well, at least L.A.," Frank corrects. "So tell me about that night."

"Keesha! Where my coffee?" he yells.

"It's coming," she yells back from the kitchen.

"Man, I already told all this to that skinny motherfuckin' Jantzen dude. Musta been at least a hundred times. Why don't you ask him?"

" 'Cause it's my case now, so we gotta start all over."

"Fuck this," he despairs.

"Let's take it from the top. You started the night off at Jackson's." She deliberately reverses the order of the clubs.

"No, goddamn, I was at the Cozy Corner. I didn't get to Jackson's until later."

Frank leads him through the times, hoping to trip him, but he's consistent. She pretends to examine notes, reading aloud, "You stopped at Sammy's for cigarettes. What brand?"

"Sammy's? I didn't go there. Shit, no wonder you can't catch this mo-fo. I stopped to the B & O for Winston's," he says, firing one up from the pack on the table.

"What else you get while you were there?"

Reginald rolls his eyes. "Lottery ticket and some scratchers."

"How many?"

"Shit, I don't know. Three, four, sumpin' like that."

"What'd you win?"

"Nothin'."

"You scratch 'em in the store or outside?"

"Outside."

Keesha brings Reginald a steaming mug.

Frank says, "Hey. Where's mine?"

The girl looks at Reginald and his shoulders jerk.

"Then what'd you do?"

"Drove around some more. Lookin' for my dawgs, Rabbit and TJ, but I couldn't find neither of 'em."

"And then?" she prompts.

"That's when I ended up at Jackson's. About six o'clock. I give up lookin' for them boys."

"Who saw you there?"

"Fuck, man, that homes a yours was always scribbling some mad shit down. Don't you got all that in his notes? And he musta taped me ten times. I know I already answered all this shit."

"I want my own notes. Who saw you at Jackson's?"

Reginald curses and Keesha slams another mug onto the coffee table.

"Thanks," Frank calls after her sulky back. She questions McNabb for over an hour. His story never wavers.

As Frank prepares to leave, Keesha complains, "You ain't drunk your coffee."

Frank winks. "I'm sure it was delicious."

Keesha blushes hard, leaving Frank wondering only *which* body fluid was in it.

Chapter 27

Over the weekend Frank makes the drive to Calipatria. William Coleman is doing consecutive nickels behind a sexual molest and aggravated assault on an eight-year-old girl. Told her he'd kill her if she told. Brave girl told anyhow and now Coleman is in solitary for his own safety.

She starts the interview by indicating the folder in front of her. "I've read your jacket, William. It looks like you're in a hell of a pinch here. Cons aren't real fond of short-eyes, are they?" He opens his mouth to answer but she cuts him off. "Point is, we might be able to help each other out. You give me what I want, I might be able to help you out."

"You gonna commute my time?"

"I'm not saying I can do that. Depending on what you tell me, though, the D.A. might be willing to work a deal. That's up to you. What I can do today, and for quite a while on, is to provide you with certain, oh, let's say, entertainments, to help you maximize your pleasure while you're in sol." Flipping the folder open, she slides kiddie porn borrowed from the evidence room across the table.

Willie reaches hotly but Frank pulls it back.

"And there's more," she coaxes. Pulling at her nose and looking at notes, she adds, "Says here you like girls' underpants. Is that true?"

The unpleasant man looks away and Frank makes a laugh.

"It's okay. You can tell me, William. Or do you like Bill?"

"Willie," he says in a voice like rats slithering.

"Willie then. I've seen it all. Been a cop close to twenty years. Nothing surprises me. Nothing disgusts me, either. To be perfectly honest, the only thing I care about is numbers. And right now, I'm working a case I can't close and that's pissing me off. You know the case, Willie." She watches his reaction when she says, "Ladeenia Pryce."

Willie looks alternately surprised and curious. She can see his mind running like a mouse in a maze. She lets it race from one dead end to the next.

"You know, Willie, this is a terrible thing to say. But I don't really care about that girl and I don't really care who did her. Or the little boy either. I see that sort of stuff on a weekly basis, and I just don't give a fuck. But you know what bothers me, Willie?" She studies him hard and just as he's about to venture a guess she answers, "The numbers. I've got a ninety-six percent case rating, Willie. Do you know how good that is? Of course you don't. But let me tell you, it's excellent. And you know what's fucking my case rating up right now? Ladeenia Pryce. I don't mean to be brutal, Willie, but I want that bitch off my books and out of my life. Do you understand?"

Willie nods.

But Frank says, "I don't think you do. No offense, but I don't think you can begin to comprehend the satisfaction of a one-hundred percent case closure. Not many people can, not even cops. Most of them don't even come close. So let me just say that I would be extremely happy, and extremely *grateful*, to whoever helps me get Ladeenia Pryce off the books. Do you know what I'm saying? I would be so happy, I'd do whatever I could to make that son of a bitch, short-eyes or not, happy. It's worth that much to me."

131

Frank pauses, pulling at her nose again. She thinks it's a Karl Malden, TV cop kind of affect a creep like Coleman might be able to relate to.

"You like girls' panties, don't you, Willie?"

Again the con has to glance away from Frank.

"I can get 'em for you." After a beat she confides, "Used."

Sick Willie flinches despite himself and the light comes up in his eyes. Frank watches him thinking, could it be true? Could it *possibly* be true?

"Don't be shy." Frank laughs again. "I know you like 'em. It says so right here." She taps the folder. "How about bras?" She suddenly lowers herself close to the table. "I can get them too. Little ones, like training bras. You like those best, don't you?"

She nods and Willie acts nonchalant, not wanting to commit himself, not wanting to believe he might actually get his hands on such contraband treasure.

"You help me and I'll help you," she whispers, leading him through an increasingly perverse scenario. Twisting his fear and monstrous lust into one pliant rein she leads Willie to that deadly Friday. She guides him through the fantasy of what he did to Ladeenia, how he caught her, how he held her, how he fucked her, and even how he killed her.

After three hours, Frank is exhausted. Sick Willie glows with insane satisfaction. She thinks him fully capable of murdering a child, but not Ladeenia Pryce. She didn't go down the way Willie claims. His story is all over the map, without one detail similar to the versions he told Noah. She maintains that her perp is a man who prefers older girls, but not knowing if she'll ever need Sick Willie again, she leaves him with the advice to keep an eye out for a package.

The deputy returns Frank's gun and she snaps it into place. She takes grim comfort knowing that even though she's been anaesthetizing herself too often and too thoroughly of late, at least a guy like Willie Coleman still makes her want to scrub her skin off.

Chapter 28

Miss Cleo calls, asking when they can meet. Frank tells her to meet her at the Tam's by the station. Resplendent in red linen, she is there when Frank arrives. Frank wonders how much time it takes Miss Cleo to get prepared for the day.

"I talked to an associate of mine. She was with Reggie a while back but she's just an old Hoover now."

A Hoover was a crackhead so down and out she'd scavenge carpet piling for rock crumbs.

"I guess you were sweating him pretty hard back then. She said it was outrageous how you kept pickin' all his girls up. It sounded like he never even saw the child you was all sweatin' him about. He made the girls he had left turn twice as many tricks and if they didn't, he'd beat them so bad they could hardly walk. That's why I've never had me a daddy. " Miss Cleo shivers in disgust. "I talked to some girls but they didn't know anything. You ask me, that boy's never hired anyone smarter than a cockroach. And that's disrespecting cockroaches."

"What else?" Frank asks.

Miss Cleo raises a slim shoulder. "Doesn't seem like there is much else. The girls he hires may be young, but that seems to satisfy his appetite."

"A'ight. What about Floyd?"

"I can't find anything about him. He's up from the Courts. Nobody here knows him very well."

"And Coleman?"

Miss Cleo flaps a meticulously manicured hand. "Don't know nothing about him, neither. I can't find anybody who's ever heard of him."

"Keep looking." Frank drains her coffee and rises.

Miss Cleo gasps. "Don't I get something for today?"

"Get me something better than nothing and I'll front you a Franklin."

Frank hasn't expected the drag queen to come up with a solid lead and it reinforces Frank's belief that Noah's best suspects are dead ends. Still, she wants to check out the last one. Returning to the office, she rereads everything Noah has on Charles Thomas Floyd.

Male, black, thirty-two. Would have made him twenty-six at the time of the Pryce murders. Noah had scratched out seven different addresses for Floyd. The latest is in Watts, at Imperial Courts.

"Great," Frank bitches. "Has to be one of the best pin-and-pops in town."

Referring to the proclivity of the project's inhabitants to pin visiting cops down with sniper fire, she debates going to the Courts alone, deciding a cold case doesn't warrant any urgency. She'll go in with a unit first thing in the morning, before the cars start getting backed up on calls and while the majority of the Court's residents are still asleep.

Floyd's rap sheet is as long as a Michener novel, involving multiple felony possessions, assaults, grand thefts, larcenies and burglaries, with dozens of misdemeanors thrown in for color. He's been sent up twice, once on AWDW and once on GTA. The grand theft auto doesn't bear inspection but Frank scours the assault with deadly weapon rap.

Four months before the Pryce case he was busted for raping a thirteen-year-old at knifepoint. The girl had stopped at a liquor store on her way home from school to buy Ding Dongs. According to her later testimony, Floyd had come on to her, mackin' and wooin'. She'd admitted to being flattered at first and had let him walk with her. Her concern started when he switched from flattery to pressure. Refusing his overtures only encouraged him. The girl became truly frightened when Floyd's pressure turned into threat, a threat he eventually fulfilled by pulling a knife on her and dragging her into an alley. He raped the girl from the back, telling her all the while that he'd cut her if she made a sound.

Floyd's history made him a compelling suspect. His alibi on the day of the abductions was weak. Only two lowlifes who'd rather fall out of a tree than tell the truth could corroborate it. Problem was, at that time Floyd lived a good sixty miles from South Central. No one could make him in the area during the requisite time frame. Along with a fistful of cousins and an uncle, Noah had unearthed Floyd's local connections. They were mostly gutter hypes and wannabe balers. None of them had seen Floyd that weekend. Half of them didn't know where he was, the other half said he'd gone up north.

Because Floyd is wanted for parole violation, she has an edge on him. She calls his parole officer and leaves a message. The PO still hasn't returned Frank's call by the time she's ready to roll after him on a foggy Monday morning.

She drives a slickback with a patrol unit behind her. She's anxious going into the projects, the building melding into the shroud of marine layer. Searching for the street number, Frank mutters, "Welcome to Shangri-fuckin'-la."

She pulls up next to a chain-link fence, assembling quietly with Muñoz and Garcia. All three scan the neighborhood. Two older women carrying grocery sacks frown at the cops, and a scrawny teenager slips into a house across the street. Mostly the fog is keeping everyone inside. Despite the weather, a whistle sounds. Curtains move aside and windows open. Frank and the uniforms maintain an even pace to Floyd's door, then knock loudly.

The adrenaline in their system makes the cops hyperalert. Muñoz hits Frank's arm. "Hey! Is that him?"

Frank turns to see an armed male black running from another building. He fits Floyd's description. Holding an assault rifle, the man pauses to unlock a primered 280Z long enough for Frank to get a good look.

"Shit!" Frank says, sprinting.

The man dives into the car. Over rising jeers and taunts, Frank hears the Datsun's engine turning over. It catches, and Frank shouts at Muñoz and Garcia, waving them toward their car.

Then the Datsun's motor dies.

Muñoz gets to the car first. Deploying to the rear, he screams at the man, "Put your hands outside the car!"

Frank sees the man turn in his seat, wide-eyed. He brings the rifle up. Garcia has already taken a knee, aiming her 9mm. As Frank hears the rifle's *ack-ack* and sees the exploding glass, she drops belly-first onto concrete. Muñoz goes down backwards, dropping his gun.

Blind fire continues from the car. Worming toward the Datsun, Frank yells for Garcia to get down but the cop is in her own world, squeezing off rounds as calmly as if she's at the range. The assault rifle suddenly stops and Frank hears one of Garcia's shots. A drawn-out moan comes from the car. Frank uses the front bumper for cover while Garcia advances.

The man sits in the front seat, strangely stiff. He stares with huge eyes at Frank. He looks like Charles Floyd. The rifle is canted against the steering wheel. Blood spills from his neck.

Frank orders him to get his hands in the air but he doesn't comply. She repeats the order, swearing, but Floyd moves only his lips. With Garcia covering, Frank yanks on the driver's door. Floyd's eyes follow her, hugely terrified.

Again she yells, "Hands up!"

Floyd squeaks, "I can't move."

Sizing up the neck wound, Frank has to decide whether Floyd's telling the truth or not. The rifle butt is only inches from where his right hand lies on the seat. Frank aims point-blank at Floyd.

"Get your fucking hands up," she speaks slowly and deliberately, "or I'm blowing your fucking head off."

"I can't," Floyd yelps again, the horror in his eyes genuine.

Careful not to place herself between Garcia and Floyd, Frank darts in. Jamming her Beretta against Floyd's temple she swipes at the rifle.

She backs away with it. Floyd still hasn't so much as twitched. Frank smells the stink of her own sweat, feels it running onto her ribs. She grabs Floyd's left arm and pulls him to the concrete. He cries out but still doesn't move and Garcia has him cuffed in seconds.

Frank tells her to call for an ambulance and backup, even as another unit squeals into the complex. Muñoz is sitting up, holding his hand against the blood seeping through at his shoulder.

"I'm okay," he breathes as Frank runs to him.

"Good." Frank grins. "Might take a while for the ambo to get through traffic."

"Especially if the natives hear a cop's down."

Frank would rather have Muñoz lie down and stay quiet until the EMTs arrive, but that doesn't seem like the safest policy after having just shot a man in the Courts. Now that the firing has stopped the residents are emerging from their apartments, their voices building to a familiar wail about rights and police brutality.

"Think you can get up?" she asks Muñoz.

"Yeah, I think so."

Frank steadies him under his good shoulder and helps him to the backseat of his car.

"I haven't sat in back of one of these in a long time," he jokes.

Angry faces press closer to the squad cars and Frank is ecstatic to see the yellow paramedic truck racing toward her. She turns Muñoz over to one EMT and follows his partner to Floyd. At least who she thinks is Floyd. She wants to ask him, but he's unconscious.

Chapter 29

A sultry dusk has settled over L.A. by the time Frank and Garcia are cut loose from the Glass House. They have spent the day at headquarters, taking drug tests, filling out reports and talking into tape recorders. They are the only ones riding the elevator and Garcia yawns. "I can't remember where I parked my car."

"I'm close," Frank says. "We can drive around until we find it."

"Thanks. I don't want to spend my night here too."

"Ever been up to the sixth floor?" Frank asks as the doors open.

Garcia shakes her head. "Not for anything like this."

They circle down two levels until they find her car. Stopping behind it, Frank tells the cop, "You did good today."

Garcia ducks her head at the praise. "I just hope Moonie's okay."

"Old Moon." Frank flips a hand on the steering wheel. "He probably stepped into the round just to get some time off."

They'd gotten word that Muñoz had a through-and-through that missed his lungs and neatly exited a centimeter left of his shoulder blade. Tore up some muscle but he'd be fine. Floyd was okay too— minor nerve damage that had left him temporarily incapacitated. Frank had been relieved to hear that, too, hoping a healthy Floyd would be less likely to instigate a tort suit against the department.

Garcia smiles. Despite her obvious exhaustion, she seems reluctant to leave Frank's car.

"Do what they say," Frank advises. "Talk to the shrink. Even if he's an idiot, it's good to spill your guts to someone you're never gonna see again. Spill it at BSU and leave it there, or it'll come back and bite you in the ass. It's gonna bite you anyway but it'll go down easier if you get it out."

Listen to me, Frank thinks, *the poster girl for the vocally challenged.*

Garcia's nodding. "Yeah, okay." She still doesn't make to leave.

"You okay?" Frank asks.

"Yeah."

"I'll give you a ride home. It's no big."

"No, I'm okay." Seeming to marshal her strength, the young woman adds, "It's just been a hell of a day."

"Yeah, it has. Go home, take a shower, get some sleep. Try to."

"I keep seeing his face, like a picture, you know, all framed in broken glass. I just keep seeing it."

"Yeah. You will for a while."

"After I cuffed him and Haystack got there I had to throw up. It kinda hit me then, you know?"

Frank nods, leaving silence for Garcia to fill.

She does, flashing a weak smile. "I guess we were lucky, huh?"

"Lucky, plus you did some damn good shooting. You were like Jane-fucking-Wayne out there. I see you doing that again, I'll get you busted back down to probation."

Garcia opens the door, thanking Frank for the ride. Frank waits until Garcia pulls out of her space then follows her from under the building.

The Alibi is only of couple blocks away and Frank gets there on autopilot. The soft evening riffles her hair and she smirks. "I should get a fucking Oscar."

When she was dispensing advice and letting Garcia talk, she felt like she was outside herself looking in. She was two Franks—one compassionate and supportive, the other detached and mechanical. She can dispense "atta girls" and sage counsel to her staff but she can't muster it for herself. Bottom line is, she's an awful hypocrite. She should be doing exactly what she'd told Garcia to do, but instead of talking the day out, she will ooze into a shot glass and clamp her mouth shut. Keep it all in. Stoic the Magnificent rides again. She knows today is going to kick her ass farther down the line, but right now it's hard to give a fuck. She'll worry about farther down the line when she gets there.

Chapter 30

Tuesday morning Frank has the shakes so bad she can't hold her coffee during the drive to work. When she walks into the station Romanowski slams the desk phone down and yells her name. Everything is too loud.

"This is a citizen with good timing," the sergeant booms, waving a slip of paper. "Got a cold one for ya."

Frank snatches the paper and heads upstairs. She used to get to work half an hour, an hour early. Now she slides in at 0558 like the rest of the squad. Jill's late, as usual, so Frank hands Lewis the paper. She's paired Jill and Lewis during Johnnie's absence, and after a five-minute briefing the detectives head to the address Romanowski gave down. Frank follows in her Honda, hoping the drive will clear her head. The chain of events from a couple drinks at the Alibi to a full-blown drunk is unclear. She doesn't remember getting home but must have driven herself, since the Honda was parked safely in the driveway this morning. The thought that she might kill herself while under the influence doesn't scare Frank, but the thought of taking someone else out with her makes her stomach roll over.

The nine-three detectives pull up to another broken body on the pavement. Hispanic male. No ID. He looks like a wino. When the coroner tech turns the body, Frank, Lewis and Jill spot the drag marks. It's a dump job. Jill and Lewis moan at the same time.

Frank tells Lewis, "It's a religious case," and Jill rolls her eyes.

"Huh?" Lewis screws up her face.

"Gonna take an act of God to clear this one."

"Shee-it," Lewis complains.

There is no evidence to collect, no witnesses to question, and Frank is soon headed back to the office. She stops at Shabazz for bean pie and a large coffee. The food eases the worst of her hangover and she drives south toward Freeman Medical Center. She still has questions for Floyd.

She finds him in a room with a large Asian family crowded around an old woman. The television blares news. Floyd is on his back, eyes closed.

"Hey."

When he sees Frank, he closes them again. She waits, reading his mood. He seems resigned, as he should be. After the hospital he's going straight into lockup, probably until he's walking with a cane.

He looks at her again and she asks, "Why'd you shoot?"

"Didn't want to go back in."

"I wasn't gonna bring you in. I just wanted to talk."

" 'Bout what?"

Holding up the well-worn pictures of Trevor and Ladeenia, she scours Floyd's face. It's blank, then changes to puzzlement.

"That's those two kids got murdered. I already been asked about that."

"Not by me. I want to hear your story."

"Man." He sighs like a tire losing air. "Ain't nothin' to it."

"Humor me," Frank tells him. "You ain't goin' nowhere."

He sighs again, bringing a forearm over his eyes. "What do you wanna know?"

Frank tries tripping him up, like she did Noah's other suspects. Like McNabb's, Floyd's story is consistent straight down the line. She's done with her questioning when she spies a tear gliding down his temple.

"What did you do that you thought I was gonna bring you in for?"

She watches his throat work as he swallows tears. He shrugs and winces at the motion. "Coulda been anything. I ain't no choirboy."

She nods and moves to the door.

Emotion makes his voice shaky, but the words are compelling enough when he calls after her, "But I ain't killed no children."

After putting in her time at the office, Frank bolts at two sharp. She's going home to work out. No stops at the Alibi. No stops at the liquor store. Frank's answering machine indicates she has two messages. One is a solicitation. The other is Gail. She tells Frank she has packed her things in a box and left it in the hall.

"Please come by and get it and leave my key on the table. If you don't want the box, please leave my key anyway."

Frank has tried not to think about Gail. She's hoped this will somehow pass. That maybe time can reconcile them. Frank knows she's wrong and Gail's right. She's willing to make a few concessions and hasn't expected the finality of this message. She plays it back. Gail sounds cool and determined.

Frank thinks about calling to offer contrition, but Gail's tone doesn't brook reconciliation. And Frank won't beg. She made her choice when she walked out and Gail made hers when she'd said don't come back. Apparently, she was serious. Frank respects Gail's resolve, wishes her own were as solid. Dropping hard rock CDs into the player, she sweats in the gym for hours, afraid of what will happen if she stops. The exercise and one tumbler of Scotch get her to sleep. But they don't keep her there.

She wakes up at three and prowls around the Pryce binders,

refusing to let Gail into her thoughts. She goes in early and a ne
glected desk keeps her occupied. Finishing the day out she leaves
around three. On the freeway, she dials Gail's number. When the
machine picks up, Frank disconnects. She drives to the apartment
and lets herself in. The box is in the hall, but Frank looks around
anyway.

Newspapers and medical journals are strewn on every available
surface alongside folders and loose papers. Coffee cups and half-
finished water bottles perch where Gail left them. Neatness was
never her specialty. A wan smile crosses Frank's face, like sun trying
to come out in the face of a hurricane. As quickly as she thinks of it,
Frank dismisses the idea of leaving a note. What would she say?

Gail's cats rub against her legs, pleased to have company in the
middle of the day.

"Fucked up, didn't I?" she says, squatting to stroke them. She
resists a wild urge to go into the bedroom and lay her head on Gail's
pillow. "Take good care of your mommy," she tells the cats.

Frank takes the box and leaves the key.

Chapter 31

It's a big horn night. Frank loads Houston Person and Terence Blanchard into the player tray. She adds Phil Woods and early Joshua Redman. Blanchard starts off on a track with Diana Krall, who begs Frank to get lost with her. Frank is happy to comply. She raises the glass that has become an extension of her hand.

Arranging her length along the den sofa, she borrows a line from the chief.

"We've made some mistakes, but this is the opportunity for rebuilding ourselves in the desired image."

Frank reviews the two things she knows for sure about police work. The first rule is that everybody lies, which in turn leads to the second rule. A good cop doesn't let shit get to her. These are the golden rules that all the academies in the world can't teach. These lessons have to be learned through on-the-job training.

Frank's been a good cop because she can maintain emotional distances. With one parent dead and the other insane, detachment was a skill Frank developed as a child. Police work honed her innate abilities, demanding that she be emotionally objective, hypervigilant, and in control at all times. Being a cop was the perfect occupation for Frank. Shit dripped off her like rain off a fresh wax job.

At least it used to. Frank swirls the rusty liquid at the bottom of her glass, descrying the crystal to track when she started slipping. Probably with the Delamore case. Rule number two kind of took a backseat when she began discovering one dead girl after another. She lost it a little on that case, and then let her guard down even more with Kennedy.

Frank wags her head. Seeing the company shrink seemed to help, but Frank should have known better. Indulging a weak moment, she'd created hairline fractures in her armature. By the time Placa Estrella was killed Frank's armor had considerable chinks in it. She and Noah, and a lot of Figueroa cops, had known Placa since she was an infant. She was a kid with a lot of promise and her murder had been hard to detach from. Frank lost any remnant of objectivity when it turned out one of her own detectives had killed the girl.

That, Frank concludes, was the pivotal moment. Instead of shoring up her reserves and sealing the cracks in her armor, she had only widened them by turning to Gail. They were starting to date around that time and Frank couldn't resist the doc. Gail was warm and funny, quick to laugh and quick to anger. Blowing into Frank's stale environment, the doc was as fresh and honest as an ocean breeze. She completely stripped Frank's defenses.

Sinking her head back into the couch, Frank pronounces, "That's where I lost it. Bought into those pretty green eyes and Betty Grable legs. What a stunner. Bitch had me tore up from the floor up."

Even though she's killing another fifth, Frank nods soberly.

"Hella mistake."

Time has shown Frank over and over that she isn't built for love. Love is for other people. Normal people. Frank is hard-wired for two purposes and two only. One is to work. To solve homicides. This is what she does. It's what she's good at.

The second is to drink. This is also what she does, and what she's good at. Raising her glass into the air, she adds, "And getting better every minute."

She knows she's drinking too much again, but this time she has planned it. Yes, she'll pay in the morning, but Fubar's on call and that's too good an opportunity to waste on sobriety. She wants to drink quickly, to get to the click, but paces herself in order to minimize the inevitable hangover.

"Should eat," she says, and gets up to peer into her desolate refrigerator. She makes peanut butter and jelly on stale bread, wondering how Johnnie's doing. He should be back soon and she realizes she's been glad he was gone. Having him around is like looking in a mirror.

Frank takes the sandwich into the living room. She forces it down with gulps of Scotch. "Sweet and Lovely" spills from the speakers. It's one of the songs she and Gail danced to the night they made love for the first time. Frank feels like a red-hot poker has been rammed down her throat. She can't breathe around the pain in her chest. She is sure it will suffocate her. And is equally sure that wouldn't be such a bad thing.

Chapter 32

The call comes in next afternoon just as Frank is leaving for the Alibi. Lewis catches it and leans into Frank's office. "Hey, I gotta go look at a possible and Jill's out talking to a wit."

"Who else is out there?"

"Nobody."

Frank swears in her head but says, "A'ight. Go get a car. I'll meet you downstairs."

Their silence is thick as they drive up to a crumbling apartment building. Paramedics are stowing their gear. Frank follows Lewis to a doorway flanked by patrol officers and neighbors. Inside a woman is screaming and kids are howling. Frank steps around clothes, toys, plastic diapers and dirty dishes. The squalor is oppressive and Frank is pissed at being called out so close to end of watch.

In the kitchen, a toddler lies on cracked and peeling linoleum. Its face is so badly burned Frank can't guess at a gender.

Garcia's the responding officer and Frank asks her, "Boy or girl?"

"Boy, Lieutenant."

The kitchen floor is slick with oil. The kid floats on it.

"What's the story?"

Garcia looks at her notes. "One of the kids ran next door, to a Martina Morales, in apartment five. She couldn't understand him at first because he was screaming but she finally got that his mother had burned the baby. Mrs. Morales ran over and saw this. She called nine-one-one and they called us. The mother claims she slipped while she was taking the oil off the stove. Says it was an accident."

Frank checks the pattern of bubbled skin. It starts at the kid's head, where most of his hair is peeled off. The blistering has obliterated his face and deformed his shoulders. She studies the spill pattern. It's concentrated in a thick pool near the body. Dabbing two fingers in the spattered oil Frank rubs them together. She shakes her head, lamenting, "Should've used Crisco. Less greasy."

Lewis blows up to Frank like a gust of wind. "That was uncalled for, LT." She keeps her voice low, but Lewis's outrage is loud enough. Frank pivots to give the detective her full attention. Anger colors Lewis's face, which is square in Frank's. She adds, "You're talking some cold, disrespecting shit. Lieutenant."

Lewis's *cojones* amuse Frank, but she has sense enough to know a smile will only fuel Lewis's fire. She can almost feel the heat coming off her.

"Right you are," Frank admits. Lewis holds her glare and Frank shrugs. "Sorry."

"Tell him," Lewis says, tipping her head toward the kid. She wheels out to the living room. Frank is left with the boiled body and Garcia, who looks everywhere but at her commanding officer. Frank sees Lewis take the neighbor aside. She follows her detective into the next room and listens. Frank is suddenly tired and Lewis is asking good questions. She leaves the apartment, grateful for the relatively fresh air outside.

Frank waits outside against the black-and-white, the sun heavy on her closed lids. Lewis was right to jump her case. Frank ponders what's happened to her—when she got so callous—but can see no defining moment. Frank knows she's hurting. And doesn't know what to do with the hurt. She can't tackle it head-on like the shrinks and Gail would have her do. She's got to come at it sideways. Sooner or later she'll get a handle on it, but right now it twists and squirms inside her like a slippery knife blade. It's easier to shut it all out, turn off everything, rather than feel anything.

The hardness is easy after so many years. Law enforcement, especially in the relentlessly murderous divisions, exacts its pound of flesh from those who pursue it. The most common blood sacrifices include divorce, alcoholism and apathy. If these aren't enough to break a cop, the toll escalates to bitterness, rage and not-infrequent suicides. Frank considers which rung of the burnout ladder she's on and thinks of Noah.

"Bastard," she whispers.

He's the lucky one. Noah got out while he was still whole. She wonders if the endless glut of human ugliness would have ever gotten to him. The Pryce case did in the beginning and she was glad when Joe finally put him back into full rotation. He resumed sleeping and eating, and Frank knew he was all right when he started whining again. She couldn't imagine the job permanently beating him down and was glad she'd at least been spared seeing that. Maybe it never would have happened to Noah. Tracey and the kids were his lifeline. They kept him afloat in a sea of shit. And it was Noah that had kept Frank's head above water. Without him, she wonders if she is drowning.

When Lewis emerges from the building Frank pushes off the car and calls her over. "First, I'm sorry about what I said in there. You were right. I was absolutely outta line."

"It surprised me, is all. It's not like you to—"

"Second thing," Frank interrupts. "This is a slam-dunk. Tell me why."

"Well, the mother says she slipped. You ever slipped with even a tiny pot of oil? Shit goes *everywhere*. You be wiping it outta the crack of your ass for weeks."

This earns Lewis a tight but legitimate smile.

"And the worst mess on that kid is from the top of his head down. Not random like you'd expect if he got spattered in a spill. That bitch *poured* it on her kid."

Frank nods, pleased. "You gonna bring her in?"

"Yeah, I'ma bring her in!" Lewis says, indignant.

"When you get her calmed down ask her two things—*why* she was moving a vat of boiling oil off the stove, and *where* was she going to put it?"

Lewis writes this down.

"Did the kids see anything?"

"Nuh-uh."

"A'ight. Look, I got an appointment. You need me here?"

"Nah, I got it, LT."

"I'll have Garcia stay with you. Let her talk to the kids. You be nice to her and she might be your partner someday."

"Or my detective," Lewis says with a sly smile.

"You plannin' on replacing me?"

Lewis blushes, explaining, "Yeah, see, 'cause you gonna be my captain."

Her detective's passion is a balm to Frank, who smiles for the second time that afternoon. "S'all good to the gracious," she says with a slap at Lewis's shoulder. "Call if you need me."

Chapter 33

What Frank neglected to tell Lewis was that her appointment was with a highball glass. Traffic on the I-10 is knotted and while Frank inches along she worries about going native.

"I was off the rim," she confides to the windshield. "That's bad when a D-I has to boot my ass."

The Crisco remark might be something she'd say behind a pitcher of beer with the boys, but certainly not on scene. Frank strives for respect with the rankest of victims and she's instilled this into the nine-three. It creates a professionalism that Frank completely lacked today. And when she swung on Johnnie.

Meandering through the last couple months, she logs other instances. She embarrassed Bobby with a castrated banger that had bled to death, joking in front of the mother that she was glad she wasn't going to have to make a cast of the wound. Then there was the incident with Miller, provoking the bastard to swing so she could get in his face. Bobby'd seen that one, too.

Embarrassment blooms in the forefront of Frank's consciousness. It's a new sensation, and one she doesn't want to get familiar with. She stares at the camper mired next to her. A young white male sits behind the wheel. He's thin and stubbly. French or German, Frank thinks. They're big on renting campers. The guy's stuck in downtown L.A. traffic with no clue where he is.

"Maybe I've got no clue," she mutters. Maybe she should talk to Clay. He's retired now from the department's Behavioral Science Unit, but before he pulled the pin he sent a letter informing her he'd be available for limited private practice. Frank can't remember if she saved the letter.

She checks out the camper again, thinking that's the answer. As soon as the Pryce case blows over she'll take a leave of absence and get her head back on. Rent a camper and travel around the states. Except for some extraditions and chasing leads down, she's never done any traveling. It might be good to see the big old U.S.A.

But the possibility occurs to her that she might never close Pryce. Frank is good, but she's not a magician. Some cases just never come off the books. Noah was a good cop. He worked it hard for over a year and got nowhere. In the six intervening years, they still haven't discovered the primary scene or uncovered one witness. The paucity of physical evidence they started with has disappeared and, barring a miracle, any unrecovered evidence will have long since followed. Odds are, lacking a credible confession or other wildly lucky break, the case may well remain a whodunit.

Unpalatable as it is, Frank has to admit this eventuality. The thought adds to her grim mood and she wishes she'd bought a pint for the road.

"Jesus." She shakes her head. "What a fucking drunk."

She turns the radio up. Sig alerts and sky cams won't do her much good now. She changes bands, pulls in KROK. Recognizes R.E.M. and keeps scanning. Jammin' oldies. Minnie Riperton. Please. She stops at The Beat. Her fingers dangle over the steering wheel and she bats them on the dashboard to an old Tupac song.

"Baby, don't cry," she mouths along. "Got to keep your head up."

Lewis's outraged face looms again and she recalls the reproach in Bobby's eyes, sees the wariness in her other detectives. Maybe she's outplayed her hand. Maybe she's so beyond burnout she doesn't even know it.

She didn't used to be like this. She doesn't want to be a relic, x-ing days off the calendar until she collects a watch, but on a day like today leaving sounds good. Take early retirement and travel around. Get the fuck out of Dodge while the getting's good. Maybe she'll do like Steinbeck, only without the dog. Travels with Lieutenant Franco. She'll visit the house in Kansas that Truman Capote memorialized. Trace the shooting spree Mailer chronicled in *Belly of the Beast*. Maybe write a travel guide to homicide in the U.S.

The camper eases past her and she thinks about what she'd take with her. Except for a couple changes of clothes, her CDs are all she really wants. After twenty years in this town all she has to show for it is what she can hear on any good jazz station. Frank mulls this over and tries not to be depressed. She studies the camper, figuring what sort of mileage they get these days. She remembers the *I Love Lucy* episode where Lucy and Ricky and Fred and Ethel piled into an Airstream and headed out West. She'd love to see the inside of one of those. She imagines lazy breakfasts in roadside diners. Waitresses with beehives pouring Folgers coffee at Formica counters.

Formica counters.

"Holy fuck."

Formica countertops. With the metal stripping around the edges. The camper in the Pryce pictures. The kitchen when you walk right in the door. Confined quarters. Take Ladeenia on the table. Spill some coffee, knock the sugar over. Bruise her leg against the edge of the table. Take her against the stove where she burns her thumb.

"Holy fuck," Frank repeats, throwing the Honda into neutral and jerking the parking brake. She scrambles through her briefcase, finding the picture.

A Mercedes behind her bleats, trying to get Frank to advance another twelve feet. Frank ignores the imperative. She scrutinizes the photo. It's the long shot from the dumpsite. Six vehicles down from the photographer, barely visible behind a work truck on the south curb, is a truck with a cab-over camper. Frank stares and the Mercedes' driver leans on her horn.

Frank moves into the space without even looking from the picture. Noah had checked every vehicle on the street. The camper had stood out because it was parked three blocks from where the owner lived. The brother of one of the women Noah had interviewed on tape. The woman who watched Oprah every day and bitched about having to feed her family. And her brother visiting from up north. Frank swears, wishing the murder books weren't on her dining room table. She tries to quell her enthusiasm. Noah would have teased it out if there was something worth teasing.

Wouldn't he?

Noah had interviewed the brother and marginal notes seemed to indicate he'd dismissed him as a potential suspect. Frank dredges the mud in her brain, trying to remember what Noah had written. She exits on the closest ramp and works north to Pasadena. The twenty-minute drive still takes almost an hour and Frank is so hyped when she gets home she forgets to pour a drink. She doesn't even unload her belt or pockets before flipping through the murder books. She can't find the obscure notation and has to go through the notes again, slowly.

There it is. Antoine Bailey. Sister said he was with her all day. Went to the grocery store in the morning, watched TV together and played Mexican Train all afternoon. Noah had run Bailey through the system, coming up only with minor vehicular infractions and traffic misdemeanors. An addendum to his notes showed Noah talked to the brother ten days later. He was on disability, an electrician by trade. Traveled back and forth between his folks' place in Bakersfield and his sister's in L.A., where he collected his check once a month.

"Don't get your panties in a wad," she tells herself. "It's probably nothing."

But she lays out Ladeenia Pryce's autopsy photos. She studies one in particular. The closeup of the bruise on Ladeenia's leg.

The bruise is shaped like the ribbed edge of a Formica tabletop.

Chapter 34

Frank is in the squad room long before the rest of the crew comes in. She can't call the Disability Insurance office until eight so in the meantime she runs Bailey through the system again. His name pops up on two priors. One's a lewd and lascivious charge about two years after the kids were murdered, and the second is a dismissed assault only seven months old. By 9:00 AM she has tracked Bailey through the DI records. His check gets sent to an address in Bakersfield. Frank cross-references the address to Kevin and Sharon Ferris. This doesn't surprise her.

She knows from knocking on doors that a Mexican family now lives in the house that the Ferrises used to live in, and from listening to Noah's tapes last night, she remembers Sharon Ferris saying her parents moved up to Bakersfield after she got married, leaving her the house on Raymond Street.

Bailey had his DI checks sent to Ferris when she lived in L.A., and now the checks go to her in Bakersfield. Frank wonders if Antoine is close to his older sister, what their relationship is like. Why the sister and not his folks? What's the bond there? Is she backing him where his parents won't? What's the hook? Frank has to find that out and work Ferris from that angle.

Ferris has two sons. She tracks one to Bakersfield, at an address not far from his mother. The second boy still lives in South Central and has accrued a variety of misdemeanors. Nothing serious and probably nothing worth riling his mother about. From the tone of Noah's interviews, Frank decides Ferris isn't friendly with the law but not openly hostile either. This gives Frank a slim edge and she drums the desk with her fingers. She hasn't felt this good since she saw Izzy Miron putting his dolls to bed.

She spends most of the day garnering information about Bailey, his sister and their family. At end of watch she hits the highway, catching I-5 to Bakersfield. Traffic is stodgy and Frank listens to the Ferris tapes over and over.

Bailey's story is consistent with his sister's. It was rainy. They spent the day together watching TV and playing dominos. In the morning they got groceries. A checker from Ralph's verified Bailey was in the store around ten that morning. She remembered because he was persistently and irritatingly macking on her. The next day he left town. He'd explained that his camper was near the site because he and Sharon had heard about some children getting killed and wanted to see for themselves. It was a shame. That's why their parents had fled L.A. When crack hit the streets they couldn't stand it anymore. They didn't want to spend their old age worried about getting hit on the head and jacked for a Social Security check. Leaving Sharon and her kids with the house, they moved up north, back to their farming roots. Antoine stayed with his sister until her husband kicked him out for not carrying his weight. Antoine stayed with his folks until the father gave him his old pickup. Antoine had been living in it ever since.

"Duh, right there all along."

She speaks aloud, wondering how many times she and Noah looked at the picture with Bailey's truck in it. What shift in vision or altering of the cosmos allowed her to connect the dots? Why couldn't either of them see the camper six days, six weeks or even six months ago? Why does it take six years for her to finally see it? Frank admits to tunnel vision with a van or SUV-type vehicle. She'd even allowed for a work truck but she associated campers with retirees or avid fishermen. Frank marvels at the hologram effect of clues. They can be hanging right in front of your face, but until you have a shift in perception you can't see them.

She comes into Bakersfield around five o'clock and heads straight to Ferris's address, noting only one car in the driveway. She finds a 7-Eleven near a Mickey D's and buys two beers to wash down a Big Mac. She eats in her car then locks up and walks around the block, giving the Ferrises time to get home from work and have dinner. While she ambles, she considers Bailey's relation to his sister. Taking in a store window gaudily displaying items for "$.99 or less!" Frank mutters, "How do we approach her?"

Frank hears herself and is embarrassed. She moves on, musing that she's getting as bad as a street person. Yet she is dimly aware, and comforted, that the "we" included Noah.

The sun dips into the horizon and Frank returns to the Ferrises' house. When she knocks on his door, Kevin Ferris doesn't look surprised. She follows him into the kitchen where his wife is doing the dinner dishes. He may not have been surprised to see Frank, but Sharon Ferris is obviously startled.

Frank introduces herself, using the time to note how Ferris's eyes dart back and forth between Frank and her husband, how she's wringing the dishtowel.

"I see you're busy," Frank says amiably. "I won't keep you long. Just a couple things I need to ask about your brother."

"My brother?" A pulse starts jumping in Ferris's throat.

"Antoine Bailey. He is your brother, correct?"

Ferris nods. She turns away, attacking a baking dish in the soapy water. "What's he done?" she asks.

"Why do you think he's done something wrong?"

Ferris glances sideways at Frank and shrugs. "Why else would you be here?"

"Do cops usually show up at your door asking about your brother?"

Ferris is silent but her husband asks, "Look, Lieutenant, what's this all about?"

Frank nods but doesn't answer. By keeping the Ferrises waiting for her response she maintains control of the conversation.

"All right," she says at length, feigning cooperation. "I won't beat around the bush with you. Antoine's in trouble."

Sharon Ferris stops scrubbing. "What kinda trouble?"

"He's facing some pretty serious charges."

"This got anything to do with them kids they found murdered?"

Bingo. It's significant that after all this time, that's the first trouble Ferris thinks of.

"I'm not gonna lie to you. It does."

Ferris assumes a defensive posture, hips against the sink, crossed arms guarding her chest. "Antoine ain't had nothin' to do with that."

"When was the last time you saw him?"

"When he come for his check. He's on disability. He comes by once a month."

"What was he driving?"

"Same as always. His truck."

"Does he still live in it?"

Ferris nods.

"He still have the same camper shell on it?"

"Maybe."

"Yes or no, Mrs. Ferris."

"I don't know." She flaps a hand. "I think so. He ain't said nothin' about a new one. He ain't got that kinda money."

Giving no sign of her delight, Frank indicates a chair. "Can we sit?"

Without waiting for an answer, she pulls the chair out. Ferris grudgingly takes the opposite seat. Her husband remains propped against the wall. Frank chooses her seat knowing Ferris will sit as far from her as possible, thus placing Frank between Ferris and her husband. Aware of the bad blood between Kevin and his brother-in-law, Frank doesn't expect Kevin to move to his wife's defense. He hasn't yet and he doesn't now, compelling Sharon Ferris to face Frank as well as her own husband.

Frank focuses Sharon. "Going back to the day those children came up missing. You're pretty insistent that Antoine had nothing to do with it. Tell me why."

"He just didn't."

Frank flicks an indulgent smile. "You're gonna have to give me more than that. Tell me about that day."

"Am I under arrest?"

"God, no." Frank fakes a laugh. "Nobody's under arrest here. I'm just trying to find out what happened to those two kids. Trying to rebuild the day."

"It was a long time ago. I can't remember that far back."

Frank reads a little from her notes to jog Ferris's memory.

When Frank asks if that's what happened, Ferris says, "If that's what I said, then I guess it must be."

"So he just hung on you the whole day. Never went to the bathroom, never went to his room."

"He didn't have no room. He slept in his truck."

"So is it possible he went out there at some point in the afternoon?"

"Yeah, it's possible."

"Possible or he did?"

"I don't know. He ain't a two-year-old. I wasn't watchin' him all day."

"So he could have spent some time out in his camper that day?"

160

"Yeah, sure. Of course he coulda."

"Did he? Do you specifically remember him being with you every minute of that day?"

"No, he wasn't with me *every* minute."

"When wasn't he with you?"

"I don't know. I can't remember."

"You just said he wasn't with you every minute."

"Well, it don't make sense that a grown man would be hanging on his sister's skirts all day. I mean, at least to relieve himself he wasn't with me. Sheeshh." She shakes her head.

Frank has noticed that Mrs. Ferris keeps a mean house. On her way in, she also noticed an ashtray by the front door. "Does your brother smoke, Mrs. Ferris?"

"Smoke?"

"Cigarettes. Does he smoke cigarettes?"

"Yeah, he smokes."

"Pack a day? Half a pack? Two packs?"

"I don't know. Maybe a pack. Pack an' a half."

"You let him smoke in the house?"

"No, I do not. He and Kevin both have to go outside. I don't like that stink in my house."

"So when he visited you down south, did you make him go outside then, too?"

She offers a nod but nothing else.

"Man smoking a pack a day must have been outside a lot. It was pretty cold the day those kids were killed. Did you sit outside with him?"

Ferris shakes her head.

"So your brother was alone outside fairly regularly throughout the day."

"I guess. That don't mean he did nothing."

"No, it doesn't. But it also means you can't protect him as much as you'd like to. There were considerable portions of the day that he wasn't with you." Frank leans forward to drive the knife in. "I know

161

he's your younger brother. The good news is, he doesn't have a prior history for this type of thing. We might still be able to help him if he's willing to talk. I'm sure you want to help him and the best way to do that is by finally being honest. Tell me why you're protecting him."

Ferris's eyes flit from Frank to her husband.

"He's my baby brother."

"And he's a grown man. You just said so yourself. Why do you worry so much about him?"

She bristles. "I ain't worried. Twan just always been different, is all. He's always been sickly. Nervous-like. But he's a *sweet* man. Brings me flowers every time he comes to collect his check."

"How do you mean he's nervous?"

"Like irritable. Like he lets little things get to him that wouldn't bother regular folks."

"Give me an example."

"Like telling him what to do. He always take it the wrong way and get all up in your face about it. He's sensitive, is all. Always has been. You just have to be careful how you talk to him."

"Must've been hard for him when he was a kid."

"Yeah, it was. He was skinny too. Other kids used to pick on him, beat him up regular like. Me and my other brother was always having to look out for him."

"Did he have friends?"

"A couple here and there. None that ever lasted long. Like I said, he was nervous and it kinda made him hard to get along with."

"How about now? Has he got any friends? Any buddies he hangs out with?"

"Nah, he ain't got no regular friends."

"Where's he stay when he's not with you?"

"Oh, he visits our parents. They's over to Visalia now. He travels quite a lot. Likes to see things. He's always telling how he was at Yosemite or this place or that. He's smart. Twan likes history. Always

162

watching the History Channel and visiting monuments and historic places. Places I ain't never even heard of it, but he likes 'em."

Frank sits back, letting Ferris's affection work for her. "What else does he like to do?"

"Oh, he can fix just about anything. I'm a liar if he didn't rewire this whole house! And ain't nothing with an engine gonna be broke for long if Twan around it. Ain't that right, Kev?"

Behind Frank he grunts, "Uh-huh."

"So he's good with his hands."

"Oh, yeah," Ferris says with sisterly pride.

"How's he take his coffee?"

"His coffee?" she echoes, derailed.

Frank nods.

"He likes cream and sugar."

"Good."

Frank moves on. She asks more questions, pushing the knife deeper and deeper into Bailey's sister. At last she sits back and sighs dramatically. She fiddles with the pencil in her fingers. She doesn't look at Ferris.

Finally the woman's anxiety crescendos and she asks, "You think he did it? You think he killed them two children?"

Blowing noisily between puffed lips, Frank says, "Let me just say, if Twan was *my* brother, I'd be scared."

Ferris starts to cry. After six years her defenses are finally breaking. Frank moves in for the kill. She rests a hand on the woman's arm.

"Sharon. Your brother needs help. I know you've tried your best, but it's out of your hands. This is too big for you. Antoine needs professional help. We've got a lot of evidence suggesting your brother was involved with those two children."

Frank refrains from ugly words like *murdered* and *killed*. She stresses there is hope for Antoine. She plies Sharon's weakness as a mother and responsible older sister.

"We also have a lot of evidence suggesting he didn't *mean* to, that it was an accident. He's never done anything like this before and as far as we know he hasn't since. But he's a ticking bomb, Sharon. Men like this can hold it inside for years before they act again, but we know, we see it over and over again, that sooner or later they're bound to do this again. They can't help themselves. Usually they don't even want to, but it's a compulsion. They can't stop it, no matter how hard they try. No matter how much they hate what they're doing. They can't stop without help, and if this goes on much longer, it might be too late to help. Is that what you want? To know you could've helped Twan but you were too afraid?" Frank bends her head to Sharon's, her voice a caress. "Is that how you're gonna help your baby brother?"

Frank doesn't move until Ferris sobs, "I don't know what to do."

"I know. I know you don't. That's okay. You've done the very best you could do and it's over now. You don't have to keep trying. Turn it over to people who are trained to help him, who can deal with this kind of problem. That's how you can help him now. It's how you can love him and protect him."

"It's like you said, I know he didn't mean to. I *know* it. It had to been some kinda accident. Whatever happened, I know Antoine didn't mean it to. He's a *good* boy."

"I know," Frank assures, thinking of Trevor Pryce taped and helpless, watching Antoine's assault on his sister. Sharon Ferris is at the flash point. Frank's job is to convince her she can help her brother. "I don't think he's bad either. He just needs help."

Ferris nods. "Yeah. He just needs help. He'd never hurt no one. Not like that. Not little children. Not my Antoine."

When Ferris wipes her nose and pleads, "What do I do?" Frank conceals her elation and shows only compassion for Antoine Bailey's plight.

Chapter 35

Frank hasn't expected it to be so simple, but Sharon Ferris is tired. Once she caves, the rest comes like an avalanche. There are no spectacular details, no smoking guns, just a long, dreary account of Antoine Bailey's restive existence. The incessant wandering, his inability to keep a relationship, the family's increasing suspicions about his activities. Sharon knows he isn't kind to his girlfriends.

He'd briefly dated a friend of hers, as well as two other casual acquaintances in the neighborhood. None of the word that got back to Ferris was good. Her brother had a bad temper. He was violent. He could be cruel, in bed and out. He didn't care about other people's feelings.

Frank listens to Ferris for more than two hours, concluding within the first five minutes that the woman's beloved brother is a sociopath. Yet Frank is compassionate and understanding. By the end of their third hour, Sharon Ferris has her name on a statement. She has put into writing what she has held back for six years.

On the day the Pryces were killed, Antoine and Kevin had gotten into an argument at the breakfast table. Antoine had helped himself to a third helping of bacon and Kevin grumbled, "You gonna eat like that you better start paying for some groceries."

Antoine retorted, "You begrudgin' your own brother-in-law his sister's good cooking?"

"I'm begrudgin' that I already got two boys to feed and I don't need to be shoveling food meant for their mouths into your belly."

Antoine whined, "You a cheap son-of-a-bitch, Kevin. Always was."

Kevin threw his napkin down and stomped from the room. Sharon tried to calm him before he left for work but couldn't. He told her that Antoine either had to carry his own weight or get gone, and the latter would be preferable.

While Antoine watched her do the dishes she suggested he should apologize for calling Kevin cheap, pointing out that he did feed Antoine and let him stay at his house every time he came to get his check.

Antoine twisted the comment around, the way he always did, putting it on Sharon that she was siding with Kevin and they just wanted him gone. Sharon tried pouring oil on troubled waters but eventually rose to the argument, ending by cursing her brother as lazy and good for nothing. Antoine slammed out the door, accusing Kevin of turning Sharon against her own kin. Antoine then spent most of the day in his truck, coming in at suppertime to bolt two huge portions and announce he'd be leaving in the morning.

Ferris saw him once more that night, when he came in around 11:00 PM to take a shower. Antoine stayed in the shower so long Kevin remarked he was going to use up every last drop of hot water and wouldn't that reflect in the electric bill. Antoine slept late the next morning, which he didn't usually do. Sharon fixed him lunch and he took off a little while later. Sharon heard about the children that afternoon. She had an uneasy thought and quickly buried it. It resurfaced when she told Antoine that the cops had come around.

He made her put together a story, convincing her he'd be a logical scapegoat for the murders just by dint of being a black man and homeless. Plus, he admitted, he had some other business—nothing bad, he'd assured her—that he didn't want the police sticking their noses into. Sharon agreed, eager to put her doubt in the back of her mind. And there it had festered until Frank came along and lanced it like a boil.

After six cold years, the Pryce case is resurrected. Ferris has copped to the story her brother asked her to tell when Noah started snooping around about the camper. Bailey has no alibi for significant time frames in the Pryce case. This is excellent supporting evidence, but in and of itself useless. Frank still needs to materially connect him to the case. Her enthusiasm that Bailey still has his original camper is tempered by the amount of time that has passed since the kids were killed. The odds of recovering useful evidence from the vehicle are slim to none, but Frank is anxious to compare the surfaces in Bailey's camper against the bruise on Ladeenia's thigh.

She debates putting his vehicle description in the box, but the case isn't critical enough for an APB. He doesn't know he's wanted and Frank wants to keep it that way. She told Ferris that if she has second thoughts and thinks to warn Antoine, it will only hurt him more than help. She gambles Ferris will keep her mouth shut, hoping the combined relief of off-loading her secrets and of duty to Antoine will keep Ferris silent.

Besides, he'll show up soon to collect his check. His pattern is to arrive a couple days before it's due, expecting the check to be early, surprised when it's not and furious if it's late. When he shows, Frank will be there with a search warrant. She contacts Bakersfield PD. They are grudgingly cooperative, agreeing to notify her of Bailey's arrival and accompany her when she serves the warrants.

Frank waits patiently for Bailey to surface. When she's not on the clock she's at home studying the Pryce books. A bottle of Scotch is never far from her hand. Reviewing the SID reports for perhaps the fiftieth time, she bemoans the lost Pryce evidence. Frank thinks what she wouldn't give for it and wonders where the hell it ever ended up. If she just had it and could reprocess it, maybe they'd find a tiny smear of DNA this time. Something the lab might have overlooked on its first go-round. Something to put Bailey away with. Or exonerate him. Either way it would be conclusive.

"Yeah," she offers to the drink in her hand. "And if wishes were horses we'd all ride."

She considers searching through Property one last time but hasn't the hope or the stamina to spare in some wild-ass chase. She'll have to build her case with what she has. But as improbable as it is, Frank still has one last ace up her sleeve.

Chapter 36

One of Bailey's old girlfriends still lives in the hood. Frank talks with her. She reiterates what a girlfriend Frank tracked to San Francisco has said.

"Front, back, sideways, upside down. That boy was just plain freaky. And he *always* wantin' some. Three, four times a day. Sometimes more. He wasn't *never* satisfied."

"What happened if you didn't give it to him?"

"Depends. He'd sulk or mope around sometimes. Most times he'd just take what he wanted. Just throw me down and do what he liked."

"Whether you were willing or not?"

"Hell, yeah." She snorts. "Didn't matter what I wanted."

"Why'd you go out with this guy?"

"He was nice at first. Used to bring me flowers and candy. He was real gentleman-like at the start. Then he just got rougher and meaner. Disrespectful. I just thought it was, you know, a mood, or something that would pass. But let me tell you, it didn't pass. It weren't no *mood*."

"Will you fill out a statement for me?"

"Hell, yeah, I will. You investigating him for something like this, I know you are, else you wouldn't be axing me all these questions about how he like it. Hell, I'll testify against that nappy-headed motherfucker any day. Motherfucker threw me into a wall before he left. Chipped my tooth, see?" She lifts her lip to point at a jagged front tooth. "I had a pretty smile, too."

"Still do," Frank says, showing her own. It's a satisfying moment when someone's willing to testify.

Frank heads to the county courthouse with Bailey's warrant. She's called ahead to check the schedule of Judge Moses Braun and catches him after he's recessed for the day. He's particularly sympathetic to cases involving children and signs Frank's warrants without even reading them.

On the third floor she runs into a cop she used to patrol with. Pausing in front of her, he needles, "I'll be damned. If it isn't Lieutenant Six Flights Up."

The man has built a career out of mediocrity and she shoots back, "If the hats aren't calling you upstairs, you aren't doing your job."

"You really knock one of your own men out?"

"Come on," she pleads. "Do I look like I could knock a cop out?"

Frank is tall, and despite her liquid diet she has maintained her gym muscles. Leaving the cop pondering her question, she continues to the DA's office. Frank has to wait twenty minutes before Lydia McQueen bursts from her office like a fire hydrant under too much pressure. Short and stout, she even looks like a fireplug. She stands in front of Frank, demanding, "What do you want?"

"Good to see you too."

Frank highlights the warrant request, citing Bailey's history of aggression, assault and forced anal intercourse. She also notes a detailed timeline of his whereabouts during the afternoon of the murders and his blown alibi.

The Queen warns, "It sounds thin."

"Thin, but inculpatory. If I can get into the vehicle"—she flaps her search warrant—"I hope to match the girl's bruise marks to the edge of the tabletop."

"Let me see that," she says, holding out a well-tended hand. Leafing through the papers, she repeats, "It's still thin. This is the best you can do after six years?"

"It was a dump, Lydia. I'm happy to have this much."

The Queen is puzzled that one of the items Frank is looking for are Ladeenia Pryce's panties. "You can't expect to find these after all this time."

"Maybe, maybe not." Frank elaborates on Bailey's pathology, explaining the possibility that he might keep souvenirs from his victims. The panties never turned up anywhere else and Frank hopes that's why.

The attorney grunts and shakes her head. "Looks like a one-on-one, Frank. The sister's word against his."

"I know."

"So why should I waste time filing based on just this?"

Frank offers her most ingratiating smile. "Because we've been working together since before either one of us had a gray hair and because you know I'm good for more. Because I hardly ever come to you until I've built a case. But mostly, because I need this guy."

Frank and the DA eye-spar.

"Even if I do sign off, you'll have a helluva time at the arraignment."

"Let me worry about that. Just get me started."

"You better find that underwear," the Queen bitches, but she puts pen to paper.

Frank is happy. After certifying and duplicating warrants, she celebrates at the Alibi. To make the evening even nicer, Nancy is there. Frank drinks, flirts and thinks only of catching up to Antoine Bailey.

Chapter 37

Frank doesn't know where she is. She stands in complete bafflement and cracks her shin on what feels like a coffee table. She thinks maybe she's in her living room, but there's no tell-tale light from the street. She shuffles with her hands extended and bumps into a padded chair. She doesn't have a padded chair. Fighting frustration and a pounding head that does nothing to clarify the situation, she gropes for a wall. She runs into another table and things clatter to the floor.

An overhead light splits her skull. She squints into it to see Nancy holding her robe closed.

"What's going on?" the waitress asks.

"Uh . . . sorry. Just trying to find the bathroom."

"Over there." Nancy points to a door in the opposite direction.

Holy shit, Frank thinks, gulping water from the sink. What in hell is she doing here? She splashes water on her face, flinches when she sees herself in the mirror. Her hair's a snake pile, her eyes are red and puffy, and there's a deep crease on the cheek she slept on. Passed out on, she corrects.

She takes some comfort that she at least woke up with her clothes on. Frank stares at her ruined face. She just meant to have a couple drinks, not end up passed out on Nancy's couch. For a horrific instant she sees how far out of control her drinking is. Queasy, she returns to the living room. Nancy has straightened the overturned table and offers Frank aspirin.

"No. Thanks. I think I'd better get going."

"Your car's not here."

Frank lets that filter through the jackhammer in her head. "I'll call a cab. I'll wait outside."

Frank looks for a phone, but Nancy sighs. "Let me get dressed. I'll give you a ride back to the bar."

"No, Nance. It's . . ." Frank glances at her wrist, amazed that it's almost five. "Okay," she relents.

While Nancy dresses, Frank combs her hair with her fingers and fills her pockets with what she'd emptied onto the coffee table the night before. Or the morning before. All she can remember is drinking stouts with Scotch backs and slowing to just stout when the anchorman on the evening news developed a Siamese twin.

Taking the stairs from Nancy's apartment, Frank asks what time they left the Alibi.

"You closed it."

"Was I obnoxious?"

"It'd be easier if you were."

"Why didn't you call me a cab?"

Nancy stops to face Frank. Pity and anger alternate across her face. "I thought maybe I'd finally get lucky last night, but you passed out while I was making the bed."

Frank is mortified. "Nance, I'm sorry."

"Yeah."

Nancy continues and Frank stays a step behind. They are quiet in the car, until Frank tries her tired excuse.

"It's not you, Nance. You know that. It's me."

"Oh, I know." She laughs falsely. "It's *always* you. But how come you're good enough for Kennedy? Or the coroner? How come you're good enough for them but never me?"

"They're different. You know that. Kennedy's a cop. We went though some shit together and then we had a fling. Is that what you want? A fling?"

"What about the coroner? She's not a cop."

"Exactly. She's not. And do you see me with her? You know how we are. You hear us after a couple beers. We're not a nice bunch of people, and it takes other cops to understand that and put up with it. The truth is, you're great. You got a lot to offer the right person, and believe me, a lotta times I've wished I was the right person. But I'm not."

"How would you know if you never tried?" Nancy snaps.

Frank sighs. "You're a civilian, Nance. Your life revolves around your son and hanging out with your friends and watching reality TV. My life *is* reality TV. I spend sixty hours a week dealing with the worst people can do to each other. I see things I don't want to tell a decent person about, things no one should ever have to hear about. What do you think we'd have in common? What could sustain anything between us?"

"Sometimes it's enough just to be with somebody warm at night."

Frank closes her eyes. The pain inside her head is preferable to the pain outside. Keeping her eyes closed, she listens to Nancy sniffle. "Look. I don't remember what happened last night. I don't know what I did. If I led you on I am truly sorry. I was drunk. I was wrong. I never meant to hurt you, Nance."

"Oh, yeah, I know. Because I'm so *nice*."

Frank doesn't know what else to say. When they get to the bar, she says, "Thanks for the ride."

Unlocking her car, she half expects Nancy to chase after her. She doesn't, and Frank blows lights all the way to the station. Because it's preferable to her shame, Frank nurses her irritation with Nancy. There's never been more than a mild flirtation between them, but suddenly Nancy's acting like they're the lesbian Romeo and Juliet.

"Fuck her," Frank swears. "Just absolutely fuck her and the duck she flew in on. Fuck Nancy. Fuck Gail. Fuck all of 'em."

She's still fuming as she changes into a clean suit in the locker room. Her blouse is wrinkled but will have to do. She dry swallows a couple naproxen and brushes her teeth.

Smacking her cheeks, watching blood replace the pallor, she murmurs, "Christ. I'm as bad as Johnnie."

She says the words, but refuses to believe them.

After a perfunctory briefing she retreats to her office and closes the door. She curses under her breath at the knock that immediately follows. "Yeah."

Lewis pops her head in. "Can I talk to you a minute?"

Lewis is barely off detective probation and Frank regrets she's been neglecting her. Waving at a chair, Frank answers, "Always. S'up?"

Lewis delivers Frank two neatly typed 60-days.

"Got an ID on the religious case?"

"Nah." Lewis flops a meaty hand. "Still a John Doe."

While she's got Lewis in her office, Frank decides to confront a nagging concern. "I hear you and Freeman been knocking boots. That true?"

Lewis is so taken aback she forgets to be angry. Then she remembers. "Who the hell tolt you that?"

"Heard it a couple different places. If you two think you're being discreet, you're not. You're a senior officer, Lewis. He's a patrolman. I hope it's worth it."

"We ain't doing *nothin'*," Lewis shouts. "*Damn*! We went out a couple times. That's all."

"Might want to limit it to that. You know the regs about mixing it up in the ranks. Wrong person gets wind of it, even if there's nothing going on, might end up in your package."

"God *damn*," Lewis complains. "How the hell a girl supposed to find somebody? Can't date a cop and cops the only one who understands when I run out at three in the morning and don't call for two days. *Damn*."

"Don't go out of pocket on me, Lewis. I don't write the rules. I'm just telling you what they are. You can go places. You got the brains and the backbone. You want to risk it all on some joystick, that's your business. Just don't say you weren't warned."

"It's not like that," Lewis insists.

"Whatever. I'm just telling you. Word's out." Frank turns her attention to Lewis's follow-up reports.

"*Damn*," Lewis repeats on her way out.

Frank wants to tell Lewis to not even bother, that sooner or later the romance will end badly. She should just concentrate on her career, because at the end of the day, especially in this line of work, that's all she'll have. But even this is not true, and Frank wisely keeps her counsel.

Over the next few days, she checks in frequently with the Bakersfield PD. If she lived there she'd be surveilling the Ferrises' place every night. Being this far away, all she can do is wait. Frank reinterviews Sharon Ferris's old neighbors. None of them have anything to add about Antoine Bailey. She helps Diego with a messy banger case. The nine-three has three unsolveds in a row and Frank wants to break the cold streak. She stays late at the office and doesn't drink. She avoids the Alibi but knows she'll have to eventually face Nancy.

She goes by after a Saturday afternoon spent at the station. She's been sober all week and allows herself three drinks because it's the weekend. She's surprised to see Nancy, who usually works weeknights. It's slow, but Nancy lets the new girl wait on her. When Nancy is alone at the bar, figuring a tab, Frank approaches her.

"Hey. You ever gonna talk to this asshole again?"

"Hi," Nancy says without raising her head.

"Look. I'm sorry I was such a—"

"Save it, Frank. I don't need your apology. I don't need anything from you."

Squaring her tabs together, Nancy drops them into her apron and leaves Frank at the bar.

Chapter 38

The stack of rented movies doesn't hold her attention. She tries reading but can't concentrate. She's finished dinner and the dishes are done. She walks circles in the den after shutting the stereo off. All her music is irritating tonight. She's feels like she's got crabs under her skin.

She makes a pot of decaf and pores over the Pryce books, pacing all the while. But eventually even they lose their grip on her. She has her suspect. All she can do is wait him out. She's already had a grueling workout, but Frank returns to her punching bag. She savages it for almost an hour. The assault leaves her soaked and weak. She thinks maybe she can sleep now. After her shower she rewards herself with a nightcap. Just one. But it's a big one.

A sergeant from Bakersfield PD wakes her at three-thirty. She's pleased about waking Fubar to explain where she's going. Double-checking that she has the warrants, she begins the easy drive north.

She slaloms through light traffic, wind blowing through the car. L.A. recedes and the stars emerge, hard and bright. She falls back to Gail's irrepressible enthusiasm about the stars, how they were shining before she and Frank were born and how they'd be shining long after they were dead and gone. Gail found their continuity reassuring. Frank only finds it depressing.

Watching the blacktop unroll in the path of her headlights, she plans how she'll play Bailey. Frank is wound tighter than coiled steel. Like a tiger stalking a deer, she's deferred hunger for opportunity. She's waited for the perfect moment to strike, and that moment is approaching at eighty miles an hour. One misstep and the prey gets away.

She coordinates with the Bakersfield boys. They park near Bailey's camper. In the new dawn, she knocks on his thin metal door. When he answers, she dangles the search warrant. She tells a stunned Bailey that she's looking for stolen property. She's looking for Ladeenia Pryce's panties, so that's partly true. Frank drops the warrant loosely to her side. By not drawing attention to it, she hopes Bailey will disregard it.

He protests, "I ain't stole nothin'."

"Well, let's just have a look," she says. Swinging into the doorway, she forces Bailey to jump down. Frank steps inside. Behind her, Bailey jabbers about harassment and planting evidence, just like they did to O.J., but in Frank's head it is quiet. This is her moment.

Though the camper reeks of stale grease and cigarettes, it is clean. Frank lays her hand on the built-in table to her left, aware of an old-fashioned, diner-style sugar dispenser. She studies the metal finish encircling the Formica. The same material girdles a narrow counter opposite. Frank pulls a picture from inside her jacket. When she smoothes it against the table, she sees her hand is trembling. There are four smudged lines in the bruise on Ladeenia Pryce's thigh. There are four raised ribs in the metal band. She holds a small ruler against the table edge. The ribbing corresponds roughly to the spacing on Ladeenia's bruise, and Frank gets shaky.

"Easy," she whispers, her voice as thin and gray as the light seeping through the curtains. She shifts her focus to the rest of the camper, wondering what else it might be hiding. She puts the picture away and allows a quick smile before hopping down to join Bailey.

"What did you find?" Bailey demands.

"What should I have found?"

"Nothin'," he insists.

"I still need you to come downtown and fill out a statement for me."

"A statement? For what? I ain't done nothin'."

"That's what I need you to explain to me." Frank makes a show of checking her watch. "Sooner we get this over with, the sooner you're back home. And the sooner I'm home."

"Yeah, and I'ma *sooner* your lily-white ass good. This is harassment. Plain and simple. You only checkin' me 'cause I'm a black man."

"If that were the case, Mr. Bailey, then there's a half a million other black men I could have picked on." She guides him toward the unit, explaining, "The boys'll take you in and bring you back as soon as we're done. Let's get this shit cleared up and be on our way."

"Yeah, you wanna get this shit cleared up all right, 'cause you done fucked up, white girl. You picked on the wrong nigger this time."

She slides him into the back of the unit, assuring him, "If that's true then this ain't gonna take long."

"It's gonna take long for you," Bailey fires back. "I'ma have the ACLU and the Anti-Defamation League crawling up your ass!"

The cop behind Frank murmurs, "Isn't that for Jews?"

Rolling her eyes, Frank closes the door and taps the hood. The car pulls away. She follows, leaving the second unit with instructions to impound the camper. Ahead of her, Bailey rants. It's like watching TV with the mute on. She'd requested a unit with a Plexiglas panel to separate the front and rear seats so Bailey can't ask for a lawyer en route to the station.

Frank drives into a smudgy sunrise, vaguely aware of the smell of her sweat. She's nervous but refuses to dwell on how much is riding on this interrogation. Pulling in a lungful of brown air, she tells herself, "Steady as she goes, girlie-girl."

Joe used to wink that at her as they stepped into the box. She wishes he were here. Wishes Noah was too. Maybe he is.

"Then it's time to pull a rabbit out of your ass, buddy. Help me nail this baby-fucker."

Frank tucks her apprehension away. Bailey's what she should be thinking about. Nothing else. She's got to be on him like crumbs on toast. She has to think like him and then three steps ahead of him. It's a chess game, his every gesture, nuance and word, the pieces.

Interrogating perps reminds her of the fable about the sun and the wind. The sun and the wind saw a man walking down the road one day. The wind said, "I bet I can get him to take his coat off faster than you can."

The sun thought about it and replied, "You're on."

So the wind blew and blew. The harder it blew, the tighter the man clutched his coat. Exhausted, the wind finally gave up.

"Let's see what you can do," the wind panted to the sun.

Smiling, the sun turned to face the man. She shined on him until sweat popped out on his face. The man kept walking and the sun kept beaming. Pretty soon the man stopped to wipe his face. The sun shined on and the wind started to gloat. The man walked a few steps more, then paused.

"Phew," he said, and then wiping the sweat from his brow, he took his coat off.

Based on the sister's description of his temperament, Frank had decided to work Bailey with persuasion rather than aggression. His behavior so far reinforces her decision. He didn't read the search warrant. He didn't refuse to come in. He hasn't asked for a lawyer and he's still shooting his mouth off. These are all good signs. She's just going to shine on him like a hot sun. Later she'll blow.

Bailey doesn't have an extensive police history, and without underestimating his intelligence, she believes she can manipulate his legal naiveté. And his pride. The man's gotten away with murder—and Christ knows what else—for six years, and waltzed on two priors. He probably feels pretty good about himself and Frank wants to keep it that way. She wants to make him feel confident enough to talk without a lawyer, hoping to get him so entangled in lies that he hangs himself.

The unit pulls into the police station and Frank parks next to it. "Here we go," she whispers. "Showtime."

Chapter 39

When she opens his door Bailey picks up where he left off.

"This ain't right. I want—"

"I know, I know" she interrupts loudly. "We all want a lot of things, Mr. Bailey. I'd like to win the lottery and you'd probably like to be left alone. I can't win the lottery, but you can probably go home if you just answer a couple questions for me. So what we're gonna do is take you inside here, get you a nice cup of coffee and see if we can't clean this mess up. If we can, then I'll cut you loose and you'll be on your way. No fuss, no muss, and you can start your lawsuit against me."

"I'm gonna," he mutters. "You best believing that."

Escorting Bailey through the station she maintains a running patter. Frank emphasizes getting him home and clearing this up, as if it's all a mistake that can be explained, no big deal. Frank wants Bailey thinking he can talk his way out of this jam.

She leaves him in a small interrogation room, returning with two cups of coffee. His has cream and sugar.

"Taste it," she tells him. "I think that's just the way you like it."

He does as instructed and Frank watches.

"S'okay?"

Bailey nods, suspicious. "How you know I like it like that?"

Frank pats her fat murder books. She's brought the open box of taped interviews in for effect. Indicating all these, she says, "That's just the tip of the iceberg, Mr. Bailey. I know a lot of things about you, so don't even try to bullshit me. I got a very sensitive bullshit meter. Be square with me and we can clean this mess up. Get the fuck outta Dodge." Punching the record button on a tape recorder, Frank tells Bailey, "This is for your protection. If I try to beat you up or force you into doing something you don't want to do, you can take this tape to the ACLU and say, 'See here? She made me do this.' Now let's play this back so you know it's working okay." While the tape rewinds, she slips in, "I should probably read you your rights, too, before we go any further, else that'll be something else for you to nail me with."

She verifies that the tape is picking them up clearly while Bailey says, "Damn right you better read me my rights. I know I got 'em, too."

"Yes, you most certainly do. Just so you know, you have the right to remain silent. You don't have to talk to me if you don't want to. Do you understand that?"

"Yeah, I understand."

"Okay," Frank continues. "So what we say here can be used in a court of law, and you can also have a lawyer here, if you want one. If you can't afford one, I'm not saying you can't, we can appoint one for you. You can talk to me if you want, but you don't have to," Frank reiterates in a rush. "Do you understand all this? I know we woke you up kinda early this morning and I don't always understand too much without my first cup of coffee. So I just want you to be clear that we can hang out here and wait for a lawyer if that's what you want."

On tape it will sound as if Frank's going out of her way to help Bailey, when in reality she's distracting him from the implications of being Mirandized.

"Shit, I don't want no lawyer, I just wanna get outta here."

"Me too," Frank sympathizes. Bailey's sister had mentioned that he hates Bakersfield, so she adds, "I don't know about you, but I'd like to get out of here and outta this town. Too much fuckin' dust and too many shitkickers."

The cop who's followed Frank in as a witness glares but remains mute. Frank grins at Bailey, broaching a rapport with him.

"Sorry about waking you up so early, but like I said, I just want to get this over with. So do you want to work this out? Just you and me? Do you want to give up the right to remain silent and talk this out without an attorney? Just you and me, one on one?"

Being a white cop, Frank is usually at a disadvantage when trying to gain a minority suspect's trust, but being a woman, plus a blonde, gives her a subliminal edge. Most men have enough pride to think they can con some dumb bitch, especially a blonde one. Bailey is no exception.

He nods.

"Is that a yes? You want to talk to me?"

"Yeah, I'll talk," he grumbles. "I got things to do."

As she slides him the waiver and a pen, she distracts him by asking, "Do you want to know what I was looking for in your camper?"

"I ain't took nothin' so how would I know?"

"I admire your confidence." Frank smiles. She opens a folder and leafs through it, waiting Bailey out.

"What you think I took?"

"Hmm?" She glances at Bailey.

"What'd you think I took? What was you lookin' for?"

"Pair of panties, Mr. Bailey."

"Panties?"

"Yeah. From a little girl."

Bailey laughs. "You think I stole a little girl's panties?"

"Stranger things have happened."

Bailey laughs again and wiggles in his chair, like a dog shaking water. Frank smiles. She asks simple questions. Where was he last night? Where'd he been before that? Can he produce witnesses to verify this? She lets him tell the truth. Lets him get comfortable.

Then she pushes a picture of a young girl across the table. The girl is naked on her back. She's slit all over, like a leg of lamb ready to be studded with garlic cloves.

Bailey winces and pushes his chair back.

"Found her a while back," Frank tells him. "Her clothes were folded right next to her. Real tidy. Everything was there except her panties. We know she was wearing them because she'd complained to her mother they were her last clean pair."

When Frank pauses, Bailey asks, "Why you showin' me this?"

"Why do you think?"

"You think I got somethin' to do with this?"

"Do you?"

"*Hell*, no!"

Frank knows he doesn't, but she wants him thinking she does. One of the last gifts a cop has is legal wherewithal to lie to a suspect. They can't physically coerce a perp into a confession but they can still mentally fuck them silly. Her plan is to get Bailey thinking he's wanted for various murders. If she can get him sweating about that, it might make him willing to cooperate, to admit to a lesser crime like rape.

She hands him a similar picture. Another dead girl, her intestines popped out of the gash in her belly. "Recognize her?"

"I ain't never seen her before."

"Really?"

"Yeah, *really*. Girl, why you wasting my time with this shit?"

Sliding a picture of Ladeenia Pryce toward him, Frank asks, "How about this one, Antoine? We never found her panties, either."

Bailey stares hard, for just a second, then says, "I ain't never seen her neither."

"You sure?"

"Yeah, I'm sure."

Frank nods. She hands him a picture of the Pryce site. "Ever seen this place before?"

Bailey barely glances at the picture before answering, "No."

Frank makes a loud buzzing noise and slaps the table. "Antoine, you done set my bullshit meter off! Come on, man. You gotta level with me here. Don't," she stresses slowly, "fuck with me. Or I'll fuck you back. Is that what you want?"

Antoine turns his head away.

Frank repeats, "Is that what you want?"

"No," he mumbles.

Sliding the scene photo under his face again, she tells him, "All right. Then I'ma get straight with you too." Frank taps the picture. "I got witnesses telling me you were here when they found these kids. I got your sister Sharon on tape, saying you and her stopped by here to see what was going on. I *know* you were there, Antoine. So let's start over. I'ma reset my bullshit meter, and you're gonna tell me the truth this time. Have you ever seen this place?"

Bailey checks out the photo. "I guess. Maybe. But it was a long time ago. I didn't recognize it, s'all."

"So were you there the day these kids were found?" Frank deals another photo from the deck. Trevor and Ladeenia smiling together, hugging a teddy bear.

"I guess." Antoine pouts.

"Good. What were you doing in the area?"

"I was at my sister's. Collecting my check like I do every month."

"Okay."

Frank leads him through the day and the day prior. Bailey stays close to the alibi he and Ferris built for Noah. He trips on a couple key details but doesn't notice. Frank leads him on, building his confidence, letting him reinforce his errors.

Suddenly she turns in her chair and faces him head on. "What if I told you this is all a pack of lies, Antoine? Everything you been

186

telling me so far, it's all lies. You dumped so much shit on my bullshit meter you broke it."

"Nah, it's all true. Ask Sharon. She'll tell you."

"I did ask Sharon." Frank pulls Ferris's statement. She lays it on the table where Antoine can read it. "She told me a different story, Antoine. Said you and she had a big fight that day."

"No, that ain't true. We ain't never fought."

"Never?"

"Nah, never."

"How about when Kevin kicked you outta the house back in 'ninety-two? Or that time a couple years ago when you borrowed his car without asking? How about the night before these kids were found, when your sister asked you to leave?"

"She didn't ask me to leave. It was Kevin askin' me. He always the one. He jealous is all. My sister loves me. She ain't never said nothin' bad about me."

"She's tired of covering for you, Antoine." Frank pats the statement. "It's all here. The fight. How you stayed in your truck all day. How you left the next morning. All here. She ain't backing you this time. She's tired, Antoine. Tired a watching after her baby brother."

"That ain't true."

"Yeah, it is. You know it is. Go easy on yourself. Tell me what *really* happened that day. Sharon already has, so you got nothing to lose. If you come clean now, this won't come down on you so hard."

"What won't come down on me?"

"Antoine," Frank croons. "We *know* those kids were in your camper with you. We know how you took 'em, front and back, doggy style." Still seductive, she alludes to evidence they don't have. "Got sperm all over 'em, man. You know about DNA."

"Not the boy," Bailey blurts out. "I ain't no faggot! I ain't touched no boy."

Bingo! Cool as summer rain, Frank shrugs. "Just the girl then. Tell me how she went down."

187

But Bailey suddenly balks. "I want my lawyer. I got a right to a lawyer and I want him now."

Frank's exhilaration pops like a cheap condom. "You sure that's what you want, Antoine? We can clear this up right now. Just you and me. Let's do it."

"Nuh-uh." He shakes his head hard. "I know my rights. I want a lawyer."

"All right." Frank sighs. "I'll get you one."

Chapter 40

Bailey is silent during the drive to L.A. Frank tries to get him talking but he maintains, "I ain't saying nothin' else until I get a lawyer."

She drives slowly, finding the most congested routes. She stops at a Del Taco for lunch. By dragging her heels, they get Bailey processed into County during a shift change. His paperwork gets lost. When they find it, he gets transferred to Pitchess. Then back to County.

While Bailey rides the legal merry-go-round, Frank has his camper towed to the LAPD garage. Because the case is such a low priority, it will be weeks before the vehicle is processed. Frank searches it carefully. There's no sign of the panties. Nothing that can be considered a souvenir. Frank needs more for McQueen. After his arraignment she visits Bailey in lockup.

"How they treatin' you?"

"Shit," he complains.

"How'd it go with your attorney? They spend a couple hours with you?"

"Hours?" Bailey's incredulous. "She wasn't here but ten minutes."

"That happens." Frank shrugs. "They got a lotta cases—I'm not being cold, it's just a fact—that are probably a lot more important than you. Anyway"—Frank slaps a stack of printouts—"we got your blood work back. Doesn't look good, Twan. You better give her a call. Let her know."

Bailey's eyes are all over Frank. She can almost smell him thinking. He doesn't know that any possible physical evidence was lost years ago and she lies to him with a confidence born of knowing how public defenders prioritize their schedules. There's no way a PD will get back to him this far from the pretrial.

"Anything you need in here?"

"Shit. What I need'd fill a phone book."

"A'ight. I'm outta here."

As she's leaving, Bailey calls out, "Toothpaste."

"Any particular flavor?" she answers without looking back.

"Crest. Regular."

"You got it."

Frank gives Bailey two days, letting the scum build up on his teeth. He's not overjoyed to see her, but he's not disappointed either.

"What'd your lawyer say about the DNA?"

"I ain't talked to her yet. She ain't returning my calls."

Frank pitches her ball. "You never been in here before, have you?"

"Nah."

"Antoine." Frank wriggles close to him. "You're lucky if your lawyer reviews your case five minutes before it goes to court. Look around you, man. How many people you see in here? You think each one of these bastards got Johnnie Cochran reppin' 'em? Hell, no. They all got PDs just like you. There are about six hundred public defenders in the system. Only half of 'em do felonies. On any given

190

day there are about twenty thousand people in and outta these jails. Not counting Juvenile Hall and CYA. You do the math. Soon as a PD gets one case cleared she gets slammed with three more. She ain't calling you back till you're dressed for court, man."

Frank shakes her head in disbelief.

"You're staring down two murder counts, Twan. You gonna put your faith in a stressed-out, overworked, underpaid, court-appointed PD? Man, if you just poked the Pryce girl admit it now and move on. Look at this place. It's packed so fuckin' tight the judge'll probably kick you in the ass, tell you not to do it again and make you serve six months. But you're gonna take a chance on a murder one rap over a little piece a poonannie? You're crazy, Twan. Rape's a long ways from murder."

Bailey considers this, eyeing Frank like a granny he's fixing to jack.

"Well, the good news," Frank says with a grin, "is you ain't young and pretty like that boy over there." Frank gives the nod to a delicately featured man-child, sobbing to his mama. "At least you got that going. Most you'll likely have to do is clean the shit stains outta your cellie's drawers. Could be worse."

"Just 'cause you slept with someone, don't mean you killed her," he says slowly.

"That's what I'm trying to tell you. And that's exactly what your lawyer's gonna say. Admitting to boning the girl can't hurt you in the long run, 'cause it makes you look honest. And like you said, screwing someone's a long way from killing them."

"Yeah."

Frank makes a show of rummaging through her briefcase. "I think I got a statement in here if you wanna fill one out. That'd speed things up when you talk to your PD."

"What would I say?"

"Depends on what you did, man. Did you poke her or not? Lotta guys mean to but they get nervous and can't get it up. Happens all the time. Don't mean nothing."

"Nah, that don't happen to me."

"So write that down, how you did her."

Antoine's still reluctant, but Frank wags her head at him. She chuckles. "You're *bad*, Antoine. Why you bonin' little girls? You ain't half bad-lookin'. I bet you could have most any woman you wanted."

"You got that right."

"So why some girl?"

Antoine shrugged. "Why not?"

Frank agrees, "Yeah, whatever. Parts is parts. Why don't you fill that out?" She tips her head to the statement. "Get you outta here so someone else can have your bunk."

"Yeah, I heard that."

Handing him a pen, she mentions, "Yeah, just explain real simple what happened. How it went down."

"Yeah, all right. You know, I just had a little sex with her. Nothin' else, you understand."

"Yeah, sure," she encourages. "It's not like you were out looking for her. She came to you, right?"

"Yeah, that's what happened." Bailey relaxes, crossing his legs at a cocky angle. "She come by my camper. It was raining a little out. I axed her in, thought she might want to get dry, you know. Wait out the rain. She come in. Sat on my bed, looked around. One thing went to another. She a pretty little girl. Next thing you know, I'd done it to her. She didn't seem to mind too much. Didn't say nothin' 'bout it."

Bailey pauses, checking Frank's reaction.

There is none and he continues, "I ain't no child molester, though. Nothing like that. It was just that one time. One time only. You know how it is, a man living all alone, he gets lonely. Men got needs. You know how it is. You been around, you seen plenty."

"Got that right," Frank echoes.

"Yeah, so see. It ain't no big deal. Just had a little fun with her, that's all, then I let her go."

"What time was that?"

"Oh, I don't know. Afternoon sometime. You know, when all the kids is outta school. Wasn't dark yet. She had plenty a time to get home. I don't know what happened to her after that."

"Tell me about doing her. Did you take her front or back first?"

Bailey looks sly. "Front, I guess."

"Where?"

"Whatcha mean where?"

"Well, like standing up, lying down. How'd you do it? That first time."

"Um, up against the table. Yeah. It was good." He chuckles a little, clearly delighting in the memory.

"How 'bout the second time."

"Wasn't much later," he brags. "She a pretty little thang. Took her up against the stove that time. From behind. Um, yep, I liked that, too."

"What was she doing all this time?"

"Not much. Just quiet like."

"Did you tell her to be quiet?"

"Yeah, you know, a little place like I got. Gots to be quiet. Don't want everyone hearin' your bidness."

"If she was so quiet why'd you tape her mouth?"

"Well." It's his first falter. "To be on the safe side. I didn't want her screamin' or nothin' like that."

"Did you tape her before the first time or after?"

Bailey recalls his timing. "Before, I think."

"You think?"

"Yeah, it was before. She had it on at the table, so it musta been before."

"You sure?"

"Yeah, I'm sure. You know, I know what I done was wrong. I ain't saying it was right. But I didn't hurt her. I had to tape her 'cause I known it was wrong and if somebody'd a heard us, and found me with her with my pants down . . . man, I'da been looking at statutory rape. I didn't want to get caught. I know I done a wrong thing. It wasn't right, but I just couldn't help myself. Had a lot on my mind, you know. A man's got needs."

Frank leads him through the sequence again as he fills out his statement. He admits to duct-taping Ladeenia, but insists he never saw her brother. Frank doesn't push the point. She doesn't have to. Frank doesn't have the physical evidence to back her, but she at least has SID's lab reports and photographs of the evidence. The tear mark at the end of the strip around Trevor's left ankle matched the tear marks at the beginning of the strip around Ladeenia's mouth. Whoever taped Ladeenia used the same roll of tape on Trevor. And now Bailey's sworn to taping Ladeenia.

They drink 7-Ups and she helps him finish the statement. When the deputy comes to take Bailey back to his cell, Frank stops him. She stands conspiratorially close to Bailey.

"One more thing."

"What's 'at?"

"What'd you do with her panties?"

"Ha, ha, ha." Bailey laughs. "Ain't nobody *ever* gonna know that." He laughs again and Frank smiles. The guard moves Bailey out.

"Dumb fuck," she whispers to his laughing back. She's still amazed at what perps will tell a cop. With or without the panties, Bailey has nailed himself three ways to the cross.

In her car, in the free, hot, L.A. sunshine, Frank calls Queenie and tells her about the statement. That simply, after six years, the case is made.

Chapter 41

Going through the motions of a celebration, Frank barbecues a porterhouse and opens an equally rich and bloody zinfandel. She celebrates alone, in front of the TV. The steak is excellent and the wine better, but Frank is relieved when the phone rings. She hopes it's an ugly call-out.

"This is Franco," she answers.

"Hi. It's Gail."

Completely broadsided, Frank's breath gets stuck in her throat. "Gail." Frank tastes the novelty of the word in her mouth. "What's up?"

"I heard you cleared the Pryce case. I just wanted to say congratulations."

"News travels fast. How'd you hear?"

"I ran into Jill. She was picking up some evidence."

Frank is dumbfounded, and Gail fills the silence.

"It must feel pretty good."

"Yeah," Frank agrees, thinking it should feel better than it does. She's noticing that the highs of homicide are lower, and so are the lows. The trip across the country that she'd promised herself flashes through her mind. And she knows she'll never take it.

She hears Gail say, "I still have your key. I was wondering what you wanted me to do with it."

My key, Frank is thinking. *My key*. Her brain has suddenly gone concrete.

"Yeah. Uh, just keep it. Toss it if you want. I don't need it back. You're not gonna pull a *Play Misty* on me, are you?"

"Not unless you've got Donna Mills hiding in your closet."

"No chance of that."

The silence waits for words.

"So how have you been?"

"All right." Frank's tongue stumbles. "I guess. Considering."

"Considering what?"

Frank wants to say considering she's lost Gail. Noah. Nancy. Almost lost her job. Might still if she can't get a grip on her drinking. Considering her life is careening around like a .22 on bone. Considering that she feels like the top of her head is about to fly off if she doesn't hold it down tight enough.

What Frank does say is, "Just stuff. You know. Work. Board of Review. All that."

"Have you heard back from them yet?"

"No," she answers, deftly redirecting the questioning. "How about you? How are you doing?"

Gail takes her time with the answer and Frank dreads what's coming because it will probably be the truth.

"I wish things were different."

"Yeah. I wish a lot of things were different."

"Like what?"

"All of it, Gail. All of it." Frank is torn between confessing her anguish and steeling herself against it. Habit wins and she forces a bland question. "How's your mom doing?"

"She's fine."

"And your sisters?"

"They're all fine. Everybody's fine."

"Good." Frank is nodding. "That's good." What else is there to say, except what she can't say? "The cats?"

"They're okay. They miss you."

"How do you know?"

"They told me."

"Ah." Frank's still nodding, the silence screaming between them. Even as she wants Gail to ask her back, she wonders if she could go. Nothing's changed. Frank knows she's digging her own grave and she just can't put the shovel down. So she does the graceful thing. "So. Do what you want with the key. But thanks for asking."

Gail doesn't answer and Frank summons the picture of Gail biting her lip and throwing her bob back the way she does when she's frustrated, snapping her neck and tossing the hair from her eyes. Those lovely emerald eyes.

When Gail says, "Okay. I figured I should check," Frank hears the tears in her voice. She closes her eyes. Regret, sorrow, longing— all the feelings she has no words for—hunker in her chest like stones, stones that weight her breath and entomb her courage.

Gail, she whispers in her head. *Gail, Gail, Gail.* Like a mantra. She wants to blurt how sorry she is. That she knows she's fucked this up. That it's all her fault. But then what? She'll change? She'll be better? Frank knows this isn't true and she loves Gail too much to lie to her.

She clears her throat. "So, I guess I'll see you at work."

"Yeah. I guess so." Gail's voice is pinched against the tears. "Take care of yourself, Frank."

"Yeah, Doc. You too."

Frank clings to the irrational hope that as long as they're both on the line maybe something will shift. Maybe a miracle will filter through the wire and they can work it out. But the phone dies in her hand. Frank finally hangs up when the busy signal turns to static.

Chapter 42

Six weeks have passed since Bailey was bound over on a double count of first-degree murder. The Queen was thrilled with his signed admissions, but what really clinched the case were the fibers SID vacuumed out of Bailey's camper. They were the same color and material as Ladeenia's sweater, but of course there was no evidence to match them to. Frank had been keeping Mr. and Mrs. Pryce informed of the investigation's progress, and when told about the fibers, Mrs. Pryce ecstatically produced the matching Pooh shirt that went with the sweater.

She still hadn't had the heart to throw it away. She'd sealed Ladeenia and Trevor's clothing in plastic tubs, opening them now and then to sniff the fading scent of her children. Frank gave the shirt over to SID and the fibers turned out to be a dead-bang match to Ladeenia's shirt. Case closed. Now the outcome is up to McQueen and how well her prosecutors play the jury.

Frank is sprawled on the couch, an almost empty bottle of Black

Label at her side. Since handing Pryce over to the DA's office, Frank has given up trying to control her drinking. She can't summon the monumental energy it takes to keep away from the bottle. Gone too is the will to even limit her drinking. She just doesn't have the fight for it. Giving in is so much simpler than going rounds every night only to lose in the fifth. She rides the liquid line between sobriety and oblivion, despairing of falling to either side.

But tonight Fubar is on call. She has taken the extra precaution of unplugging her phone. No midnight pleading for her to take over a scene will interfere with her drinking. She's been at it steadily since end of watch. She started with a pint of Jack Daniel's while driving home, then plowed through a six-pack of Coronas in the backyard while barbecuing hot tdogs she ate straight off the grill.

Food doesn't interest her and she forces herself to eat. Her life revolves around clawing through morning hangovers then working as long past end of watch as she can before bowing to the hunger for that first drink of the day. She's quit going to the Alibi. There's no one there she wants to drink with and Nancy is frosty.

She's taken to stopping for a pint on the way home and by the time she hits her driveway she's got a gentle buzz on. She spends the rest of the night tending it. Somewhere between eleven and twelve she's had enough to help her sleep. She swallows Advil and vitamins, brushes her teeth and wakes up around 2:30. Sometimes she can go back to sleep. Usually she can't, until she has a tumbler of Scotch. Then she dozes until 4:30, gets up woozy and starts the cycle all over again.

She is watching *Cops* with the mute on. Coltrane plays in the background, with Johnny Hartman on "Dedicated to You." She loves that song, but it doesn't touch her. None of her music sounds good tonight. Sinatra and Ella are too maudlin. The opera that can move her to tears leaves her cold. Miles, Mingus, Redman—they all make her nerves itch. Nothing can soothe her tonight. Not even the booze.

This is the terrifying thought she has been dancing around since that morning at Nancy's. What happens when the alcohol doesn't work anymore, when the tail is thrashing the dog?

Not much frightens Frank, but the thought of being unable to escape herself is more than she can handle. She swallows from her glass, as much as her mouth will hold, and repeats the motion. She watches a cop in Houston trying to reason with a drunken wife-beater. She should be smashed by now, but she hasn't heard the click yet. That lovely, comely, magical click.

" 'Did you say click?' " she whispers, quoting from *Cat on a Hot Tin Roof.*

" 'Yes, sir', " she answers in Paul Newman's drawl. " 'That click in my head that makes me feel peaceful. It's like a switch clicking off in my head, turns the hot light off and the cool one on, and of a sudden there is peace.' "

Like Burl Ives, she growls, " 'Boy, you're a real alcoholic.' "

" 'That is the truth. Yes, sir. I am an alcoholic.' "

Frank turns the glass in her hand.

"Yes, sir," she repeats in her own clear voice. "That is the truth. I am an alcoholic."

She sits with the statement, unashamed and unrepentant. Just tired. Very tired.

On the coffee table, next to her feet, rest her .38, .357 and Beretta. Each weapon is meticulously cleaned and oiled. They gleam in the TV's blue light. Each fully loaded.

Frank levels her glass between her eyes and the handguns.

"Cop on a hot tin roof," she muses through the jeweled refraction.

Colors glitter and twinkle in the crystal. She squeezes her hand and the crystal shatters. She crushes the shards into her palm. Hanging her hand over the couch she lets it bleed onto the tile floor. She considers the fiery little stabs of pain. They feel good and she tightens her hand into a fist. The shards bite deeper.

Studying her macerated palm, she notes, "You are one sick puppy."

She watches her hand until the bleeding slows, then assiduously removes the shards over the bathroom sink. She takes pleasure in the pain. When she is done she pours rubbing alcohol over her hand and wraps it in a towel. She returns to the couch with a fresh bottle of Scotch. She doesn't bother with another glass.

Unbidden, like a butterfly in a garden, a sparkling long-ago afternoon flits across the landscape of Frank's memory.

It was early in their partnership, at the start of their shift one day, when Frank and Noah got the crying-baby call. They'd pulled up at the address dispatch gave them, to a house overgrown with weeds. The neighbor who'd called in the complaint met them on the sidewalk. The man who lived in the house had only recently moved in after winning his son in a vicious custody case. The last time the neighbor had seen the man was yesterday afternoon. He was walking into his house with his son in one arm and groceries in the other. The baby had started crying around 8:00 PM. She'd thought maybe it was just fretting, but she'd heard it again in the middle of the night and it hadn't stopped since she woke up this morning.

"He seems like a good father," the woman said.

Noah thanked her and told her they'd take it from there.

Frank knocked, calling loudly, and got no response. They walked around the house and peeked through windows with drawn curtains. Seeing nothing. They kept calling and knocking, trying each lock. Finally they busted a small pane and were able to reach inside to unlock a window. Noah, the skinnier of the two, went in first, calling out so he didn't get shot for a burglar. He let Frank in the back door. Even though the sun was high and hot, lights were on throughout the house. A baby's subdued, rhythmic cry came from down a narrow hallway.

Noah, in the lead, glanced into a room off the kitchen. "Uh-oh."

A man fitting the father's description was sprawled on the floor in front of the television. It looked like he'd taken a shotgun blast to his head and neck, the resulting wounds dark and coagulated.

Frank checked cursorily for a pulse, as Noah exclaimed, "Holy fuck."

She looked up to see him backing away from a bookshelf over the TV, pointing.

"See it?"

It took her a moment to track his finger, then she saw the vacant eyes of an over-under 12-gauge aimed just above her head.

"I think we better get—" Frank's words were engulfed in a boom. Noah had fallen to the floor and Frank had flattened. They looked at each other, afraid to move.

"Did you touch something?" she whispered.

Noah searched around himself. His foot was inches from an end table.

"Jesus Christ, we're fucking booby-trapped. I got fishing line on this table going under the couch. Can you see it at your end?"

Frank tentatively crawled around the couch. She saw the line appear briefly from the couch and disappear under another table. She inched along beside it, eyeballing it up the wall and behind a shelf to another shotgun.

"Shit," Noah said, seeing the barrel at the same time. "We gotta get outta here."

Frank nodded. "Let's just crawl out the way we came in."

They crept from the room on hands and knees, hugging the floor and searching for tripwires. Frank had forgotten the baby but remembered it as they approached the kitchen. The sudden gun blast had triggered hiccupped crying.

"Noah," Frank said.

He looked behind himself, at her.

"It's gonna be hours before we get a demo team assembled and in here."

"The baby," Noah finished for her.

"Yeah. What if there's something wrong with it?" Tossing her head toward the body in the living room, she continued, "I mean, it looks like he offed himself. Either on purpose or by accident, but what if he did something to the baby first?"

"I know, I know," Noah whined, veering toward the hallway.

"Noah!"

He stopped.

"Don't move," Frank ordered. She crabbed up next to him, blocking the hallway. "Go back to the car and get demo and homicide in here. I'll get the baby."

"No way."

Noah surprised Frank by making a rush past her. He almost got by until she threw her shoulder into his ribs, shouting, "Damn it, No, don't make me kick your fucking ass in here!"

She could, too. Noah knew that and paused to consider this latest threat. They stared at each other for seconds that seemed like minutes, Frank loving Noah, marveling that he'd take the risk even as she was infuriated that he assumed the right to.

"Think it over, dumb fuck. Who's got a wife? Who's got kids? Come on. Move over. Let me do it. I'll be okay if I keep low. Besides, Tracey'd kill me if I let anything happen to you."

Noah reluctantly crawled back a few paces.

"Shit," he called after her scuttling butt. "Don't make me have to call Maggie."

Frank heard him but didn't hear. She'd seen the almost invisible line tied around a closed doorknob. She traced the line to where it retreated into the doorjamb. She didn't see a connection across the hallway and continued. Sweat tickled the underside of her arms, incongruously erotic, given her state of terror. She eyed the walls. They were lined with snapshots in cheap frames and shelves crowded with knickknacks. Anything could be rigged up there. With amazing recall she remembered every war story she'd ever heard in the Academy or patrol room about walking into booby traps.

Continuing to creep along the carpeted floor, she realized the baby had stopped crying.

Shit, she thought. *Hang in there, little guy.*

She paused at the open door to an unlit room. Reasoning that the door would likely be primed only when it was closed, she hustled past, glancing into a darkened bedroom. She was bone-jellying grateful as Noah encouraged helplessly, "You're doing great."

"Yeah," she tried to joke. "Think I'll make the back of the *Law Enforcement Bulletin*?"

"Only if you die."

"You sure know how to make a girl feel good."

She approached a third door. It was open. Frank searched for a telltale line, saw none, and proceeded beyond a brightly lit bathroom. In addition to fingering her way through the dirty brown carpeting, she remembered to check above her head. There she saw an axe head peeking from behind a high framed mirror. She had visions of it flying down at her, as if swung by demons in a horror movie.

"Jesus T. H. Christ," she mumbled, pausing on her elbows, ass low.

"What? What is it?" Noah called.

"He's got a fucking axe up there. Doesn't look like it's wired to anything, though. What a fucking nut."

"Be careful," Noah answered.

"Ain't gonna get up and tango with you, if that's what you're thinking."

"*Damn*," was the game reply. "One of these days."

"Don't hold your breath, buddy."

The ribbing calmed Frank as she faced two more doors. The one on the right was closed and she easily spotted the rigging on the knob. The door opposite was open. She sidled along the carpet, approaching the darkened doorway until she made out a crib against the curtained windows.

"Hey, little guy," she called to the baby, more to comfort herself than the baby, who was still disquietingly silent.

Using her prior logic, that an open door wouldn't be rigged, she started crawling into the dim room. Rustling, then a gurgle came from the crib, and Frank saw a lump that looked like a baby.

She stopped four feet from the crib, shouting, "Why's this guy booby-trapping his house, Noah?"

The quick answer was, "To keep his wife from stealing the baby?"

"That's what I'm thinking. So what would be the first thing you'd rig?"

"The baby's room."

"Bingo."

The lump in the crib moved, and large brown eyes looked at Frank.

"Hey," she said to the baby. "If I didn't want anybody to take you the first thing I'd rig would be your crib."

The baby stirred listlessly and Noah asked, "See anything?"

"Uh-uh. That's what's scaring me."

"Is the baby okay?"

"Looks like it."

"Frank, get out of there. If the baby's not bleeding to death or unconscious, let's just wait for demo to get him out. He'll be all right a little longer."

The anxiety in his voice belied the rationality of Noah's suggestion. It sounded like a good idea and Frank weighed it seriously. She asked, "Shouldn't the baby be crying if there's nothing wrong with it?"

"He's probably exhausted. Been crying since yesterday. A few more hours won't kill him."

Christ, Frank thought. *What am I doing here? Why didn't I just leave this for demo?*

Then she said to Noah, "In for a penny, in for a pound. Besides, I gotta get on the cover of the *Bulletin*."

"Next year," Noah whined. "Come on."

Hearing his concern, she was tempted to turn around and crawl back the way she came, but she advanced toward the crib. Stretching gently onto her belly, she swept her fingertips around the bed's legs. Then she raised an arm and fingered the railings for line. She almost pissed her pants when she touched a sprung mattress thread.

The bottom of the crib seemed safe enough, but Frank wondered how to get the baby out without standing.

"Where are you?" Noah asked.

"Right by the crib."

"Shit. Come on, Frank. Let the demo birds do this."

Frank tugged at a blanket on the floor, waited, then pulled it toward her. Waving it above her head, she prepared for a blast. None came. She waved the blanket over the crib with similar results. Still waiting for a gun to go off, Frank slowly raised herself to a kneeling position, a crouch, and then tentatively stood. She reached for the baby.

"I got him!" she yelled to Noah.

She turned with the baby against her chest just as she heard the KABOOM and felt the concussion of the blast pass her head. The blast deafened her but she felt the baby renew its crying and she lifted her head just enough to yell, "I'm okay, No! I'm okay! I got the baby!"

Not sure how she'd tripped the blast, she froze where she was. Remaining face down in the rancid, crumby carpet seemed the best option. Just sit tight and wait for the bomb boys to come. At least wait for her ears to clear, but Frank wanted desperately to be out of this room and out of this house. Her body insisted she move, but her mind demanded she stay. Paralyzed, she'd listened to the warring inside her. Eventually an overpowering need to pee had forced her to scuttle back to Noah.

Tonight, bedeviled by dead friends and lovers, haunted by busted relationships, a precariously maintained job and an incomprehensible craving for alcohol, Frank feels exactly like she did on the floor of that filthy bedroom fourteen years ago. She is terrified to move forward and can't go backward. Stasis seems the only alternative. It's enough just to keep breathing.

Frank imagines calling in sick tomorrow and staying on the couch until she runs out of Scotch. She can call a liquor store and have them deliver more. She'll write checks until she's out of money, and that'll be a long time. She has months' worth of vacation and sick time. She could just sit here until she dies or the bank forecloses and sends her to an institution. Neither ending seems unpleasant, nor implausible.

With marvelous effort she pulls herself upright. Leaning over the guns on the table, she fingers each one.

"You been with me the longest," she addresses the .38. "Outlasted everyone."

She cradles the wheel gun in her left hand.

"Remember that duster that came at me? You saved my ass that time. And that Piru that wanted to eat me for lunch? Saved me then, too. Hell, you had my back first day on the job, with that pig FTO Roper. Don't think I didn't know you were there." Trading the .38 for the .357, she tells it, "He's my boy, but you're my girl."

The barrel is long and blue, as finely turned as a beautiful leg, and Frank easily pulls Gail from her memory drawer.

"Aw, Doc. Best legs in the world. Miss Universe legs. Betty Grable got nothin' on you." Frank draws the satiny barrel across her lips, mumbling, "God, I fucked that up. Righteously and completely fucked it up."

Eyes shut, she slides the steel against her mouth. The metal warms to her touch and Frank dreams the gun is Gail. She kisses it, lightly teases her tongue around the tip of the barrel. Her aching is monstrous. She lowers the gun to her lap. It nestles like a puppy with the .38. After a long pull on the bottle she picks up the 9mm.

"And you, my friend, are just a killing machine. About as sexy as the mess you made outta Timothy Johnston's brains."

A couple years have passed since she killed the dealer in a bust gone bad, but she can still see his do-ragged skull flying up into the air. In slow motion. Some things you never forget. The Beretta joins the other guns in her lap.

She's been drinking for effect, going hard on twelve hours now, but her head and heart are sickeningly clear. Rolling the bottle against her forehead, she whispers, "Where's the click?"

She opens her eyes to the trio of weapons in her lap. Talking large gulps from the bottle, she reevaluates each weapon. The .38 is short, stout and effective. The little engine that could. Reliable, solid and friendly. She could never betray it like that. It wouldn't be fair to the gun.

But the .357. Now that's a sexy gun. Just suck and squeeze. What a fucking mess she'd make. And who'd find her? The cleaning lady? That'd be cruel. Frank would have to leave an extra big check. Probably someone from the squad would come over. Maybe Fubar would send a unit. They could handle it. Probably get some good jokes out of it, too. But as much as she loves the .357, she doesn't have a history with it. It'd be like fucking a gorgeous stranger.

The Beretta's the way to go. The 9mm is a working gun. Quick, blunt, to the point. All square edges and efficiency. Nothing personal, just business. It would understand why she chose it and be glad to do its job.

Frank puts the other two guns on the table. She leans her head back. Closing her eyes, she caresses the Beretta. She shakes the towel off, holding the gun in her right hand, the bottle in her left.

It'd be so simple. One squeeze, and pow.

Done.

Over.

Frank puts the barrel in her mouth. Savors the tang of metal and oil.

Her thumb slides over the safety, clicking it off. Her finger wraps around the trigger. Home.

The clip is full.

One squeeze.

Less than a second and five pounds of pressure.

Kaboom. Bye-bye baby. *Hasta la vista.*

Frank's heart is thudding. She can feel it in her chest like a tiger in a trap. She has the power to stop it. Forever. Like Noah's heart.

Boom. One squeeze. Game over.

Frank's hand shakes. She swallows. Her mouth is dry.

She recalls George Thorogood's line, *You know when your mouth be getting dry, you're plenty high.*

She wants to laugh. Sweat runs into her eyes and she loves the sting. She's really shaking now, her finger still curled around the trigger.

Jesus Christ. One squeeze. That's all.

Just do it.

Do it.

The barrel chatters against Frank's teeth. Sweat and blood make the grip slippery.

Pull, just pull. Quick!—and pow. Game over. Lights out.

Dandy Don singing, *Turn out the lights, the party's over.*

Frank's finger curls tighter. She considers her backdrop. All clear. Go ahead.

Pull!

Pull!

A delay in programming causes the TV screen to go black. For just a second. And in that second Frank catches her reflection, hand jumping, gun in mouth, and she is throwing up. She sweeps the guns onto the floor and pukes until she's dry-heaving, coughing up blood. She can't stop the shaking. She staggers into her room and wraps herself in the bedspread. She slumps on the floor, almost convulsing. All she can think is, *seconds and inches. Seconds and inches.*

In time her shuddering subsides and with it the terror. She feels as scoured as a beach at low tide. Dropping head to knees, she looses hot, clean tears. When they dry, she pulls the phone off the night-stand. It takes her a couple tries to hit the right numbers, but eventually the phone connects. Listening to it ring, she pleads, "Be there. Christ All-fucking-Mighty, please be there."

A sleepy voice answers.

"Hey. It's Frank."

"Goddamn. What time is it? You forget I'm not your LT any-more?"

"I didn't know who else to call."

He may be retired, but Joe barks back, "What is it? What's wrong?"

He stays on the line while Frank searches for enough guts to answer.

Joe encourages, "What's the matter? Tell me what it is."

"I can't do it, Joe. I know you did. Maybe you can tell me how."

"What can't you do?"

Frank squeezes her eyes shut. She forces the answer. "I can't stop drinking, Joe. And I'm afraid something bad's gonna happen if I don't. Something real bad."

The silence is as long as the distance between L.A. and Minnesota. When it's broken by a war whoop, Frank despairs that her connection's been severed. But then Joe's laugh is in her ear, and it sounds like he's crying when he says, "Girlie-girl! You don't know how long I've been waiting for this call!"